LOUISE'S LIES

LOUISE'S LIES

Sarah R. Shaber

MYS
SHA

This first world edition published 2016
in Great Britain and the USA by
SEVERN HOUSE PUBLISHERS LTD of
19 Cedar Road, Sutton, Surrey, England, SM2 5DA.
Trade paperback edition first published
in Great Britain and the USA 2017 by
SEVERN HOUSE PUBLISHERS LTD

British Library Cataloguing in Publication Data
A CIP catalogue record for this title is available from the British Library.

ISBN-13: 978-0-7278-8654-5 (cased)
ISBN-13: 978-1-84751-755-5 (trade paper)
ISBN-13: 978-1-78010-821-6 (e-book)

All Severn House titles are printed on acid-free paper.

Severn House Publishers support the Forest Stewardship Council™ [FSC™],
the leading international forest certification organisation.
All our titles that are printed on FSC certified paper carry the FSC logo.

Typeset by Palimpsest Book Production Ltd.,
Falkirk, Stirlingshire, Scotland.
Printed and bound in Great Britain by
TJ International, Padstow, Cornwall.

To my husband, Steve, my arm candy and champion,
thank you for everything. KBO and WOFC, babe!

ACKNOWLEDGMENTS

I owe so much to everyone who has supported my writing it's difficult to know where to start with my thanks. My family, my husband, Steve, my daughter, Kate, and my son, Sam: you are my best friends and supporters. The late Ruth Cavin was my first editor and taught me the ropes with infinite patience. My current publisher, Severn House, who turn my manuscripts into books with the personal attention and quality that is rapidly fading elsewhere in the industry. I am fortunate to be represented by my agent and friend, Vicky Bijur. Thanks to my writing buddies, Margaret Maron, Diane Chamberlain, Kathy Hogan Trochek (Mary Kay Andrews), Brenda Witchger (Brynn Bonner), Alexandra Sokoloff and Katy Munger. Where would I be without you? And how lucky am I that my home bookstore is Quail Ridge Books here in Raleigh? Bob Adler and Terrie Gale, thanks for showing me around your building, which used to be the Woodward Apartments, and for giving Steve and me a place to sleep in Washington! Mike Pearse, thank you for telling me the anecdote that inspired this book.

I appreciate my fans more than they can know. They give me the energy to keep writing Louise's story.

ONE

Saturday evening
December 11, 1943
Washington, DC

When we left the theater a powerful gust of frigid air struck us head on. It surprised us with its force, pushing us into the sandwich board that advertised Greer Garson in *Madame Curie*. As the board collapsed Joe caught it and cursed in Czech, his native language, which I rarely heard him use. The two of us together couldn't set the board upright so we let it crash to the ground and left it lying on the sidewalk. Above us the already dimmed theater marquee went dark. The nine o'clock show had been canceled.

'Twenty-two degrees,' I said, reading the temperature off the clock over the bank across the street. 'It could be worse. It could be snowing. Or pouring freezing rain.'

'I'm not ready to go home yet, are you?' Joe asked. 'Let's get a drink.'

'I'd love a drink, but so many places are closed.' Most of the citizens of the capital city had stayed home tonight, avoiding either the cold or the flu, which had already confined 80,000 people in DC to their sick beds. We'd started our evening at Joe's apartment fixing canned tomato soup and grilled cheese sandwiches for supper, but cabin fever finally drove us out looking for something, anything, to do. We'd braved the cold to see *Madame Curie*. The theater was almost deserted, as we'd expected. The soda jerk swore he'd already had the flu, and so did the usher.

According to the morning's *Washington Post* the victims of this epidemic should hit 100,000 this weekend and then taper off. I hoped so. There weren't enough healthy nurses in the hospitals to care for the patients.

The ghastly weather, painful as it was, had been a godsend.

Cold didn't kill germs, like some people thought, but it did keep people inside their homes so they couldn't come into contact with sick people.

Another good result of the cold and the flu was that the 78th Congress planned to recess for Christmas earlier than usual and spare us their constant bickering. A crowd of hotheaded Southern Democrats, pressured by Southern railroad companies, was threatening to urge various states to secede over the rules set by the Fair Employment Practice Committee, the rules that guaranteed colored workers the same wages as white employees. What nonsense, when we were in the midst of a worldwide war!

'Look,' Joe said, pointing down the street. A neon martini glass with an olive suspended in it flickered over a double door. Light poured out the transom and through the large plate glass window with *Baron Steuben Inn* painted on it. We bent into gusting wind, forcing our way down the street, and pushed through the heavy oak door.

In the vestibule we stripped off our heavy coats, scarves and gloves under the self-assured gaze of the baron himself, who gazed at us from a cheap print copied from the famous portrait by Charles Willson Peale.

'Who was Baron Steuben? I'm surprised any business in this city has retained a German name,' Joe said.

'Steuben was a Prussian officer who volunteered to fight with the Continental Army during the Revolutionary War,' I said. 'He was General Washington's chief of staff. He lived here for the rest of his life.'

'Oh,' Joe said, hanging our coats from two of the hooks that lined a wall of the vestibule. 'That explains it.' I shivered. The small space was almost as chilly as it was outside.

As we had expected the bar had few customers. Some of the tables and chairs had been cleared away and stacked in a corner between a front window and the entrance to the back of the bar. The bar stools had been moved too – so drinkers couldn't sit at the counter and spread germs, I supposed.

The warmth that greeted us as we walked inside the bar was almost as shocking as the cold. Steam clouded my glasses and I had to clean them with my handkerchief.

The few patrons who'd braved the frosty weather in search of a drink collected at the remaining tables, spaced well apart from each other. A balding, middle-aged man playing chess with himself occupied the best table, the one nearest the roaring fire. He moved a white rook, then turned the game board around and rested his head in his hand, pondering his next move. A few tables away, under the well-worn dartboard, a blonde woman wearing corduroy trousers and a heavy fisherman's sweater was reading *The Robe*, Lloyd Douglas' bestselling book about the crucifixion of Jesus. She was sipping coffee from a steaming mug; I could smell its comforting odor from where I stood. She was at least as old as I was, over thirty, I guessed, but wore her ash-colored hair long, like Veronica Lake. A chocolate-colored mink coat, real mink, not dyed marmot or skunk, was draped over another chair at her table. If I owned a coat like that I'd keep it by my side too. When she reached for her coffee I noticed a square-cut diamond ringed with tiny rubies on her right hand. The rock had to be two carats.

An elegantly dressed couple holding hands, leaning so close together their heads almost touched, occupied a table directly in front of the fire. Their cocktails sat on the table, ignored. The woman had a lovely coat too, black cashmere with a sable collar, draped over her shoulders. When her date's hand moved up her arm I saw a thick gold watch peek out from his sleeve. I wondered why they were slumming here.

At another table near the vestibule's entrance two workmen quietly sipped their beers. One wore the uniform of a Capital Transit bus driver. The other appeared to be a common laborer. His clothes were shabby and his coat was missing a button. They ate sandwiches from a brown paper bag.

The barkeep raised his hand to us. He was shockingly thin and barely out of his teens, pale with dark circles under his eyes. A sheen of moisture coated his forehead. He looked as if he'd just risen from a sick bed himself. 'Holler out your order,' he said, 'and I'll place your drinks on the bar, and when I step back you can come get them.'

'A gin martini,' Joe called back. 'Just a little vermouth, no olive.' Joe knew me well. 'Do you have any European beers?'

'Sorry,' he said, 'just Budweiser.'

'Whiskey?'

'Nope. We haven't got our order in yet.' Whiskey supplies were running low all over the country and causing a public outcry. There were rumors that the government would allow distillers to decrease their production of war alcohol so they could restock liquor store shelves, but until then buyers were limited to one bottle a week. I was glad to be a Gordon water girl. Gin didn't need to be aged.

'All right,' Joe said, disappointed. 'Whatever you've got, I guess.'

The barkeep placed our drinks on the bar and stepped back so Joe go could retrieve them and pay the chit.

'Ma'am,' said the man sitting alone with his chess set. 'I'm well over the flu. My chess partner didn't show up; would you and your friend like to join me here by the fire? I'd like the company.'

I glanced at Joe and he nodded, so we went over to his table and sat down. I sipped my martini while Joe swallowed some beer, but not without grimacing first.

'Not exactly pilsner, is it?' the man said.

'No, it's not,' Joe answered. He stretched his hand across the table and shook hands with the man. 'I am Joe Prager,' he said. 'This is my friend Mrs Louise Pearlie.'

'I'm Al Becker,' he answered, clasping Joe's hand and nodding in my direction.

'You must have recognized my accent,' Joe said.

'Of course,' Al answered. 'You're Czech, yes? Where the best pilsner in the world is brewed.' Al had a slight accent himself. German.

That put me on guard. There were plenty of innocent German speakers in DC these days, but I worked for the Office of Strategic Services in a covert section and took no chances with strangers.

'Yes,' Joe answered. 'But I was living in London when the war broke out and I carry a British passport.'

'I am an American,' Al said. 'I immigrated after the last war. I became a citizen when I married an American woman. I can't completely get rid of my accent, much to my dismay.

It marks me wherever I go. It's not good to have a German accent in America these days.'

Al picked up his chess pieces and stowed them neatly away in a battered case, folding the chessboard over the top and snapping the case closed. He sipped from his own beer.

'I don't know why I keep coming here,' he said. 'It's blocks away from my apartment. But years ago I'd meet my friends here because it served all the best German beers. I can't break the habit.'

A few feet away the elegant couple broke away from mooning at each other to sip their cocktails. The woman crossed her legs. I could swear she was wearing silk stockings and I wondered where she'd found them. Black market, probably. The man, who had a slicked-back haircut with a wave over his forehead, pulled two cigarettes out of a pack of Camels and put them in his mouth. He lit them both with a silver cigarette lighter and gave one to the woman. They leaned together again and spoke in whispers to each other. This bar didn't seem that romantic to me, but they were clearly oblivious to their surroundings.

A peal of laughter broke out from the table with the two workmen, interrupting us. The Capital Transit bus driver, who had a bald head ringed with ginger hair, stomped his foot, laughing, while his friend drained his glass, dribbling beer down his chin.

'We need refills,' the dribbler said.

'I'm sick of beer,' the bus driver said. 'I want a double shot of whiskey.'

'You heard the barkeep,' his companion said. 'There's no whiskey.'

'Maybe not for the likes of us.'

'What do you mean?' his friend asked.

The bus driver pushed back his chair with a scraping sound that attracted the notice of the elegant couple, diverting their attention from each other. The woman reading looked up from her book.

Al and Joe glanced at each other. 'Are there often fights here?' Joe asked.

'Not when I've been here,' Al said.

'Maybe we should leave,' I said.

'No,' Joe said. 'The troublemaker is between the door and us. Let's see if the barkeep can handle it.'

'The boy's been ill,' Al said. 'We might need to step in.'

The bus driver bellied up to the bar. 'Pour me a double whiskey. Four Roses, please,' he said.

'I'm sorry,' the young barkeep said. 'We're out of whiskey. We have plenty of gin.'

'I don't want cleaning fluid,' the bus driver said, 'I want a real drink, a man's drink.'

'I can't help you,' the barkeep said. 'I just can't. Please back away from the bar. I've just gotten over the flu. I'm not in good health.'

The bus driver turned and pointed to the elegant couple. 'What about them?' he asked. 'Could they get whiskey if they asked for it? Have you got a bottle back there reserved for your best customers?'

The elegant man spoke up, raising his glass. 'This is brandy, sir, not whiskey. Very good brandy indeed. I'd be happy to buy you and your friend a round.'

'I can vouch for the brandy,' the blonde woman said. 'I had some in my coffee.'

'Here,' the barkeep said, pulling a bottle of brandy off the shelf behind him. He held it out to show the bus driver. 'It's Hennessy. You'll like it.'

The bus driver clenched and unclenched his fists, as if deciding whether to stay combative or settle for a glass of brandy instead.

The blonde woman at the table under the dartboard finished her spiked coffee and shoved her book into her handbag, ready to leave if the bus driver wasn't mollified.

'Look, Walt,' his friend said to him, 'leave it be. Let's take this fellow up on his offer. I'd like to taste that brandy myself.'

Walt stared at his friend for a second. 'OK,' he said. 'But first I want to check behind the bar and see if there's any whiskey stashed away there.'

Al spoke up. 'Surely that's not necessary. I know Cal. He's an honest kid. If he says there's no whiskey, there's no whiskey.'

I could feel Joe and Al tense in their seats, ready to rush

Walt if he should become violent. The blonde woman wrapped her scarf around her neck. The elegant couple moved too, pulling on their coats. Everyone in the bar was getting ready to leave quickly or to intervene if necessary.

'Then he won't mind if I check behind the bar,' Walt said, moving toward the open end of the bar.

'Come on, Walt, cut it out,' his friend said, standing up at his table. 'We don't want no trouble tonight.'

The piled-up tables and chairs in the corner near the entrance to the bar blocked Walt's path, so he forced himself through them, picking up one chair and throwing it aside, almost breaking the front window. The barkeep, sweating profusely, blocked his way. 'You can't come back here,' he said to Walt. 'Please. There's no whiskey. I swear.'

Joe and Al jumped up, moving quickly toward the bar. Walt's friend was moving too. 'You dummy! Stop it!' he shouted across the room.

I noticed the elegant couple moving past me in the opposite direction. Headed for the back door. Didn't want to be involved. The idle rich hated seeing their names in the newspaper.

Walt forced the barkeep back easily, with just one hand, then bent under the bar to search for the whiskey he seemed sure he'd find there. But he quickly rose, his eyes wide with shock, and staggered backwards into the bottles and glasses that lined the back shelf, knocking some of them off the ledge and on to the floor, where they broke and splintered into pieces.

'Holy Mary,' Walt said, his face contorted with horror. 'There's a dead man on the floor back here.' He glanced up and repeated himself, as if he didn't think we'd heard him. 'A dead man! Soaked in blood!'

For a few seconds no one moved. Then Al and Joe dashed toward the bar. Al got there first and swung behind the counter, then covered his mouth when he saw the corpse.

'Good God,' he said. 'It's Floyd!'

'Who?' Joe asked.

'Floyd Stinson, the man I play chess with every week!' Al sank to his knees beside his friend, with a hand stretched out to touch him, but Joe grabbed his arms to keep him on his feet. 'Watch out,' he said to Al, 'there are shards of glass everywhere. You'll cut yourself.'

Walt had recovered his self-control and had pinned Cal's arms behind him. The young barkeep looked terrified. He even had a couple of tears tracking down his face.

The elegant couple had found the back door, but I moved between them and the exit. 'You can't leave,' I said. 'There's been a death, a violent one. The police will come and want to question us all.'

'Not us,' the man said. 'We're not involved. We can't be here.'

When I saw his face full on I recognized him. He was Leo Maxwell, the playboy and rich industrialist's son, who was excoriated in the newspapers when he was found 'unfit' for the armed forces despite being an avid tennis and polo player. And if my memory of the last society page I'd seen him in was correct, the woman he was with was another man's wife. She must have interpreted my expression correctly, for she pulled her sable collar up to cover her face. 'Please, Leo, let's go,' she said.

Maxwell elbowed me aside and I allowed them to leave. What else could I do? Now that I knew who the man was I could tell the police his name. The two of them swept past me and out the back door, letting in a blast of freezing air as they left.

Walt's drinking buddy was the next person to go AWOL. He pulled on his coat and hat and half ran to the front door. 'Walt, this is your fault! I don't need this, I'm going home,' he called out as he slammed the door behind him.

The blonde woman made no attempt to leave. But instead of watching the drama behind the bar unfold, she simply unwound her scarf and pulled her book out of her pocketbook. As if she planned to keep reading while the situation was resolved. She must have had no nerves at all.

I heard Joe's voice and turned back. He had Al by the arm and was leading him out from behind the bar. 'The man's dead,' he said to Al. 'There's nothing we can do for him. We have to call the police now.'

'There's so much blood,' Al said, his voice breaking. 'It couldn't all be Floyd's, could it?'

Walt dragged Cal out from behind the bar and shoved the

panicked barkeep into the chair. The boy put both hands on his chest and seemed to be having trouble breathing. 'It wasn't me,' he said, between gulps of air. 'It wasn't! I found him there when I opened up this evening!'

'And you decided just to leave him?' Walt asked. 'That makes no sense.'

'I didn't know what to do,' Cal said. 'The man was one of our customers. I was going to call the police after the bar closed. I swear.'

'Sure you were,' Walt said, raising his fist.

'Stop it,' Joe said to him, grabbing his arm. 'Stop bullying him. Can't you see the state he's in? Questioning him is up to the police.'

The blonde woman, who'd opened her book for all as if she was in her own home, looked up from her page. 'Speaking of the police, has someone notified them?' she asked. 'Wouldn't that be a good idea?'

'The pay phone's the only telephone we got. It's on the wall behind the bar,' Cal gasped out. No one seemed eager to go behind the bar where the dead man lay. And to my surprise neither Al nor Joe moved.

Of course, I thought, both men had accents. Not a good first impression when reporting a death to the DC Metropolitan Police. They were just as suspicious of foreigners as everyone else.

'I'll call them,' I said.

'Don't, Louise,' Joe said. 'I'll do it.' But I was already behind the bar. I couldn't help but see the body, but I wasn't squeamish about it. Years of gutting fish at my parents' fish camp had inured me to gore. Al was right, there was a great deal of blood. Only a very large, sharp knife could cause that kind of bleeding. And not with just one wound, either. The victim must have been stabbed several times. Before I looked away I noticed the dead man had black hair cut short and a nose that looked like it had been broken at least once. He wore overalls and scuffed shoes.

I raised the telephone receiver and realized I needed a nickel. My purse was back on the table along with what remained of my martini.

I turned to the men crowded around Cal, the barkeep. Al was fanning him with a dishtowel.

'I need a nickel,' I said.

Joe dug into his trouser pocket and tossed me a coin.

I caught it and dialed the operator. 'I need the police,' I said to her. 'There's been a murder. At the Baron Steuben Inn on Massachusetts Avenue, across from the old German embassy.'

It was a good thing there wasn't another murder or a stickup in progress. It was twenty minutes before the police arrived. We spent most of it in silence. The blonde woman calmly turned the pages of *The Robe*. Al got Cal a glass of water, going into the bathroom near the back door to get it instead of behind the bar. Walt followed him, entering the bathroom after Al came out, then emerging with damp hair and tidy clothes – trying to look sober, I supposed. Joe tossed more logs on the fire until it roared. I gulped down the remains of my martini.

I was about ready to call the police again when we heard the familiar siren squeal of a DC Metropolitan Police car and the crunch of its wheels on ice as it pulled to a stop outside the bar. Through the front window we saw another draw up behind it.

Al opened the door. In limped an older man wearing a heavy coat and a dilapidated fedora, his face hidden by the scarf he'd wrapped around his neck up to his eyes. He leaned heavily on a cane. A uniformed policeman, equally bundled up, walked behind him carrying a black briefcase. Two more policemen with their revolvers drawn followed behind them. I could hear a frightened sound from Cal, a sort of gulp and exclamation combined.

The plainclothes policeman and I met each other's eyes. I knew him immediately. He looked older and a little beat up, with more lines in his face. And he hadn't shaved today, either.

'Well, Mrs Pearlie,' he said. 'Fancy meeting you again. At a crime scene, too. Just like old times.'

It was Detective Sergeant Harvey Royal. I knew him from a drowning incident that involved an OSS employee some months ago. An incident I couldn't discuss, of course.

Royal unwound his scarf and the policeman at his side quickly pulled out a chair so he could sit down.

'Sergeant Royal,' I said, stretching out my hand to shake his. 'I'd say it was good to see you again, except . . .' and I glanced at the bar.

'Except for the corpse?' he asked, allowing himself a brief smile.

He addressed the entire group. 'I'm Detective Sergeant Harvey Royal of the DC Metropolitan Police.' He nodded toward the policeman with the briefcase. 'This is Officer Dickenson. He accompanies me everywhere because my lieutenant, who can barely shave, thinks I am too decrepit to manage on my own.'

Royal turned in his chair to speak to the policemen behind him. 'You may holster your revolvers,' he said. 'Staines, you watch the front door. Morrison, find the back door. Make sure it's secured and wait there. OK,' he continued, 'show me the corpse.'

'It's behind the bar,' Al said. 'Around here.'

Using his cane and with his right hand firmly gripping the seat of his chair, Royal pushed himself to his feet and limped behind the bar, followed by Dickenson. He stared silently at the corpse for a time, then grabbed at Dickenson's hand for support as he lowered himself behind the bar out of our sight. He seemed to stay down there forever, but then we saw Dickenson struggle to raise him to his feet. Once upright Royal leaned heavily on the counter, breathing hard.

'It had to be him,' Walt said, pointing toward Cal. 'He said he found the body just before he had to open the bar and was too scared to do anything about it. Who would do that? He's been serving us all night with that bloody thing keeping him company.'

'No,' Cal said, 'no! I swear I didn't kill him!'

Royal glared at Walt and limped out from behind the bar. 'I'll do the police work here, thank you.' He looked Cal up and down. 'You don't look strong enough to shove a knife that deep into a body,' he said.

Cal looked like he'd been drowning and someone had just thrown him a rope. 'I'm weak from the flu, too,' he said. 'I

just got out of bed today because the boss said he'd fire me
if I didn't come to work.'

'Sit down; you look like you're about to fall over. For that
matter you all might as well take the weight off for a few
minutes,' Royal said, pulling his notebook out of his pocket.
Like characters in one of Mrs Christie's stage plays gathering
in the drawing room, we all took our original seats.

'Mrs Pearlie, would you tell me what happened when the
body was discovered?'

'Why her?' Walt asked. 'I was the one who found him.'

'Because I know Mrs Pearlie,' Sergeant Royal said. 'I know
her to be truthful and pithy in her speech. Pithiness being the
most important quality. And she's not blotto.'

After I started to speak Royal interrupted me. 'You and
your friend were the last in this unfortunate little group to
arrive?'

'Yes,' I said.

'And your name?' he said, looking at Joe.

'Joseph Prager,' Joe answered.

Royal raised an eyebrow at the sound of Joe's accent. Joe
answered his implicit question. 'I'm a Czech with a British
passport. I teach Slavic languages at George Washington
University. I used to room at the same boarding house as
Mrs Pearlie.'

'Fine,' Royal said. 'Please continue, Mrs Pearlie.'

When I finished my story, Royal tapped the tabletop with
his pencil. 'Does anyone disagree with Mrs Pearlie on any of
these particulars?' he asked. No one answered. 'Good,' he
said.

Royal looked over at the blonde woman sitting composedly
under the dartboard. She had said nothing since he arrived,
just sat patiently with her finger marking the place in her book
where she'd stopped reading.

'And your name is?' he asked.

'Mavis Forrester,' she said.

'Miss or Mrs? And your occupation, if any.'

'I'm not married. I work in the circulation department at
the Library of Congress.'

'And you,' he said, looking at Al.

'I'm Al Becker.'

'The dead man was a friend of yours?'

'Not a close friend,' Al answered. 'His name was Floyd Stinson. We met each other here some months ago and have been playing chess most Saturday nights since.'

'You have a German accent.'

'I immigrated here after the last war.'

'What do you do for a living?'

'I work at the zoo. In the administrator's office.'

For a few seconds the atmosphere in the bar lightened. The Washington zoo was one place in the capital city where one could go and forget the war. I spent many Sunday afternoons there. I'd never seen any exotic animals before, and was delighted by the giraffes, great cats and elephants. I found the great apes fascinating, even though I found their resemblance to human beings a bit discomfiting.

'So, Mr Becker, what did your friend do for a living?'

'I don't know.'

'Really?'

'We just played chess. He never mentioned work.'

'Do you know where he lived? Or if he had a family?'

'I know it seems odd, but we just played chess. The only other thing I know about him is that he lived around here. I mean, he walked here.' Al paused, as if he'd had another thought he was deciding whether or not to share.

'Spit it out,' Royal said.

'I've never seen him in work clothes before,' Al answered. 'I would have thought he did office work.'

Royal turned his attention to me. Thank goodness there was one person here he could trust.

'Mrs Pearlie,' Royal said, 'you recognized one of the men who left the bar early as Leo Maxwell but you didn't know his companion?'

'That's correct.'

'I know who she is,' Mavis Forrester spoke up. 'Her name is Gloria Scott.'

Royal raised an eyebrow. 'The Gloria Scott from the gossip columns?'

'That's the one,' Mavis said. 'She's married to that Scott

boy, the one whose family owns that huge ball bearing factory in Illinois, but she doesn't let it interfere with her social life.'

'And your friend,' Royal said to Walt, 'he left too.'

'That was just Chippy,' Walt said. 'He spent six months in jail for selling ersatz gasoline coupons on the black market. He took off to avoid the police. He's got nothing to do with this.'

'Nonetheless,' Royal said. 'I need his name, address, and a telephone number where I can reach him. And all the rest of you, too. Give your information to Dickenson here.' Royal handed his notebook off to the policeman. 'Don't talk to anyone, and I mean anyone, about this. That includes your families. I'll find out if you do,' he continued, 'and you'll regret it. I'll get your official statements tomorrow.'

'Tomorrow?' Al said. 'Aren't you going to question us tonight? What about Floyd's body? Where are the police photographers and the doctor?'

Royal massaged his knees. 'Mr Becker,' he said. 'Your friend doesn't need a doctor. He's dead. After we examine the scene tomorrow his body will be transported to the police morgue and a doctor will examine him.'

'You can't just leave him here all night!'

'I certainly can. It's late and dangerously cold outside. It's not necessary to bring our people out in this. Mr Stinson can wait until morning. I'm leaving Officers Staines and Morrison here to keep him company. You,' he said to Cal. 'You run this place?'

'Yes, sir,' Cal said.

'Make sure the heat stays on so my officers can stay warm. How many keys to the doors do you have?'

Cal pulled a key ring out of his pocket. 'I have one set,' he said. 'Front and back doors. The owner has another. He lives nearby, off Scott Circle.'

'Give them to me,' Royal said, reaching for the key ring. Cal handed them over.

'Ain't you going to arrest him?' Walt asked, nodding at Cal.

'No, at least not tonight,' Royal answered. 'Where do you live, boy?' he asked Cal.

Cal pointed at the ceiling. 'Upstairs. I got a room here so I can keep an eye on things.'

'How do you get up there? From inside the bar?'

'No, sir. The stairs is outside.'

'OK. In the morning you call the owner and tell him what's happened. Tell him the bar will be closed for a couple of days. In the meantime you don't go anywhere, hear me?'

'I got to go out to eat,' Cal said.

'Then tell the patrolmen on duty where you'll be and when you'll be back. This place will be packed with police tomorrow. Stay out of their way.'

'Yes, sir. Can I go now?'

'Yeah, go on. Get out of here.'

With one swift movement Cal grabbed his coat and was out the door. We could hear him clatter up the steps and into his room overhead.

Royal levered himself up from his chair, groaning in pain. 'Goddamn knees,' he said.

We stood around him, wrapped in our coats and scarves, waiting to be dismissed.

'It's bitter cold out there,' Royal said. 'How are you all getting home?'

'I got my truck,' Walt said.

'I have my car too,' Al said. 'I live way up Connecticut Avenue, across the Taft Bridge.'

'I can walk,' Mavis said.

'How far do you have to go?' Al asked her. 'I could give you a lift.'

'It's just across the street and around the corner,' Mavis said. 'I am perfectly capable of walking it, even in winter. Good night, everyone. I cannot say it's been an enjoyable evening.' Al held the door open for her as she left.

'She's one tough broad,' Dickenson muttered to himself under his breath.

'You two go on,' Royal said to Al and Walt. 'I'll wait here a couple of minutes to make sure you can get your vehicles started.'

The two men left, leaving Joe and me behind with the two policemen.

'How will the two of you get home? Do you have a car?' Royal asked me.

'I'd planned to hail a taxi on Thomas Circle after we had our drink,' Joe said. 'Now I'm worried we won't find one at this hour.'

Just thinking about walking home in this weather so late at night made me feel weary.

'Dickenson and I will drive you,' Royal said to me. 'I can't have my witnesses frozen solid. Do you still live in the same boarding house?'

'I do,' I said, 'and Joe's apartment is just a block to the west.'

After Royal spoke to the two policemen staying behind to guard the bar, Joe and I retrieved our coats, hats, scarves and gloves from the vestibule and the four of us went outside.

The street was desolate. No one in his right mind would stir on a night like this. No sane cat, dog or mouse either, for that matter. The streetscape, lined with bars and cafés with apartments above them, appeared abandoned, like a ghost town. Every now and then I could see a second-floor window edged with a narrow band of light escaping around blackout curtains, but that was the only sign people lived here. My breath escaped from behind my scarf in a cloud of white fog, so thick I couldn't see out of my glasses, and I gripped Joe's arm. Sergeant Royal grasped a lamppost for support as he stepped off the curb, but it was so cold he had to struggle to free his glove.

Parked on the street was a Chevy pickup enveloped by a miniature blizzard caused by the heat of its idle engine meeting frigid air. We couldn't see the driver through the fog. We couldn't miss the car, though – it was painted aqua. Painted by hand, with a paint brush.

'What the hell,' Royal said. 'Dickenson, find out who that fool is.'

Before Dickenson got halfway to the car the driver rolled down the window. It was Walt.

'Just getting the motor warm,' he said. 'I should be good now.' He rolled up his window; we heard the truck go into gear and he moved down the street.

'I believe that truck is uglier than my car,' Royal said.

'No one has a vehicle uglier than that bucket of yours,' Dickenson said.

After using Royal's cigarette lighter to thaw the car door handles, the four of us climbed into a black sedan with the emblem of the DC Metropolitan Police painted on the car doors. Dickenson engaged the engine, but it stalled. After waiting a couple of minutes Dickenson turned the ignition key again, and the engine fired.

'Thank God,' Royal said.

Dickenson eased the coupe on to Massachusetts Avenue. Across the street the abandoned German embassy loomed black over its neighbors, mansions where some light seeped out from behind blackout curtains. Before the war the Germans held gay parties and dinners there almost every night. Rumor had it that the third floor was the center of a vast German espionage center and that it was packed with radio and electronic equipment. Now the Swiss minded the place, part of their role as a 'protecting nation' for the property of the European nations at war with each other. I'd heard that Hitler had promised the Swiss he wouldn't invade if they safeguarded German embassies around the world.

We swung around Thomas Circle, passing the statue of Martin Luther that had been donated to the nearby Lutheran church by the German emperor William I in 1884.

Exiting on Vermont, we turned west on 'K' Street and headed toward my boarding house. It was slow going. Since the headlights were shaded, Dickenson could only see a few feet in front of the car. The heater blasted but barely made a dent in the cold. When we got to my corner Dickenson pulled over to the sidewalk.

'You can let me out here too. I can walk to my place,' Joe said. 'It's not far.'

Royal turned around in his seat and faced us. 'Don't say a word to anyone about any of this,' he said. 'Not your roommates, not your work colleagues, nobody. I want official, signed statements from everyone who was in that bar tonight before the reporters and gossips get wind of this murder, and I want those statements to be accurate. Tomorrow's newspapers have gone to press already, so there won't be any headlines until Monday. Then the vultures can do what they want. Got it?'

'Of course,' I said.

Royal looked at Joe. 'I know Mrs Pearlie can keep her mouth shut, but can you?'

'I can vouch for him,' I said. Both Joe and I had plenty of experience keeping secrets.

TWO

Joe and I stood on the sidewalk holding hands a[s] the police car slowly disappear down the street[.] went into each other's arms and our lips met. The[n] of our kiss was a rare moment of comfort in an icy, frig[ht] world.

I'd been attracted to Joe instantly. He was already livin[g] 'Two Trees' when I'd arrived fresh off the train fro[m] Wilmington, North Carolina almost two years ago. I was struck immediately by his dark good looks, his modest self-confidence and his education. It wasn't long before I learned that he wasn't what he pretended to be, a Czech refugee teaching Slavic languages to soldiers who'd soon find themselves on battle-fields in Europe. He worked for the Joint Distribution Committee, a Jewish charity, helping Jewish refugees escape Nazi-occupied Europe. Other than that I knew little about him.

It wasn't wise for me to be in love with Joe. I knew instinc-tively that he was one of the good guys, but his Czech accent and refugee passport instantly aroused suspicion during wartime. So I hid our love affair from everyone, including my housemates and my superiors at work, to protect my place at Phoebe's and my precious job at OSS. Without my Top Secret clearance I'd be just another government girl.

'I'd better get on home,' I said, pulling away from him.

'Me too,' he answered. 'Or we'll be found frozen solid here, wrapped in each other's arms, in the morning.'

After dropping off Mrs Pearlie and her friend, Patrolman Dickenson pulled out on to Pennsylvania Avenue. 'District HQ?' he asked Royal.

'Yeah,' Royal said, rubbing his knees. He had to make his report and request a crime scene team for tomorrow morning before he could go home and take some laudanum. At the office he could down two double bourbons and toss back a

pain. That would have to

upon. A corpse hidden
se depressing movies
ell what the hell was
y. He'd have a quiet
trons. They could
s. They could be
r Louise Pearlie.
e could count on her
happened since she and
. That was something.

the front door of 'Two Trees', my boarding
Washington Circle, south of 'K' street. Inside I
off my gloves and stuffed them in my pocket but kept
my coat on. It had been a long time since dinner, and since I
saw a light on in the kitchen I went down the hall toward it.
I found Madeleine, our colored housekeeper's daughter, filling
a hot-water bottle at the sink.

'How was the movie?' she asked.

'Good,' I said. 'Very good.'

'It's late,' she said.

'We stopped for a drink afterwards.' At a dive with a corpse
behind the bar. But I couldn't talk about that.

Madeleine, wrapped in a yellow chenille bathrobe with pink
daisies strewn all over it and with a knitted watch cap snug-
gled on her head, screwed the top back on her hot-water bottle.
'My crowd wanted to go out tonight, but all the colored clubs
were closed. All we could do was get a hot dog and come
home.'

Madeleine treasured her evenings out. She and her mother
got on OK, considering they shared a bedroom in the basement, but their bedroom and the kitchen were the only parts
of the house they were free to spend time in. It was hard for
an educated twenty-year-old girl with a good paycheck to
settle for such a restricted life. As far as the DC Housing
Authority was concerned Madeleine had adequate housing.
No one would rent an apartment to a colored girl anyway.

'How are Ada and Phoebe?' I asked her. My fellow boarder and landlady had been down with the flu for a couple of days.

'Better. But we need someone else to get sick,' Madeleine said, 'so we can keep the heat on.'

After Madeleine went downstairs to her room I searched the pantry for a snack. Most everything in it was organized carefully for future meals. And I didn't dare touch anything that was rationed. In the end I found a half a packet of saltine crackers and a tin of sardines. Sardines were among the rare swimming creatures I would eat, so I added both crackers and sardines to a plate. Since the heat was on upstairs I took the plate up to snack in bed.

While I munched I thought about the remarkable evening I'd just been through. Of all the bars in DC, Joe and I had stopped in the one with a dead body hidden behind the counter! Kept secret for hours by the barkeep, a kid so scared and so puny it was impossible to think he had put it there. How long were Joe and I in the bar before the body was found? A half an hour, at most? Some of the others must have been there for hours. And if Cal was to be believed, the corpse was behind the bar when he opened earlier in the evening.

And then, of all people, it was Sergeant Royal who was running the case. He should be retired by now, what with his age and terrible knees, but the lack of young men to join the police force kept him on the job. I liked the man despite his crustiness, but I'd just as soon forget the circumstances of our acquaintance. There was a murder then too, but I'd made a serious mistake I didn't want OSS to know about, and Royal recruited me to help him investigate it by threatening to tell my bosses about my blunder. That incident had ended well for me, but I'd still rather not be reminded of it.

I edged Ada's door open and carried her breakfast tray into her room. 'How do you feel?' I asked her. 'Can you eat anything? I brought tea and toast.'

'I think I can,' she said, scooting up in her bed. Ada was fashionably dressed even when confined to her sick bed. She wore a pink-flowered flannel nightdress with a matching quilted bed jacket. Her peroxide blond hair was tucked under a pink sleeping turban. But her sallow skin and bloodshot eyes showed the effects of three days of the flu.

'I didn't have any fever this morning,' she said, tentatively biting into her toast. 'So I guess I'm on the mend. How is Phoebe this morning?'

'I don't know yet,' I said, sitting down on the edge of her bed. 'Dellaphine just took her a tray.'

'This toast tastes so good,' Ada said. She slurped her tea. 'And the tea, too. I wonder when I can go back to work?'

'The doctor said he'd come by tomorrow to check on both of you,' I said. 'I guess he'll tell you then. But you know all the hotels' public areas are closed. And it's seventeen degrees outside. I don't think you'll be leaving the house for a while.'

Ada was a clarinetist with the Willard Hotel house band. She couldn't work until the city allowed the lounges and ballrooms to reopen.

'I guess I've got some leave, then,' she said. 'Unpaid, though.'

'You can afford it,' I said. With so many young men overseas, bands were paying good money to musicians, even women, who could keep their dance bands swinging. Washington was packed with throngs of government girls, office workers, soldiers and sailors who wanted to drink cocktails and dance to the latest tunes whenever they could.

'Done?' I asked.

'Yes. Can I have some real chow soon?'

'If you feel like it I don't see why not. I'll bring you some lunch later. And the newspaper, once everyone downstairs has read it. Do you want a book? I've got a couple I can lend you.'

'I don't think so. But you can hand me my manicure kit; it's on the bureau. My nails are a mess.'

I met Dellaphine in the hall carrying Phoebe's tray, which looked as though she'd been able to eat something too.

'Phoebe's better?' I asked.

'Yes, praise be.' Dellaphine said. 'Did you know Miss Phoebe's momma died of the Spanish flu? In 1918. I'll never forget it. This sickness ain't near as bad. I hear most everyone lives through it.'

Dellaphine was Phoebe's colored housekeeper and cook. She'd been with Phoebe's family since she was a fourteen-year-old kitchen maid, and moved with Phoebe to her home when Phoebe married Milton Holcombe and set up house-keeping. Her loyalty to Phoebe was so powerful she refused to go with her husband when he quit his job as the Holcombe butler and driver to join a jazz band. Madeleine spent time with her father when he was in town, but Dellaphine adamantly refused to see him. To her it was purely stupid to leave a kind white family where a person could work a whole life and be cared for through sickness and old age. Ironically Madeleine worked for the Social Security Administration, but Dellaphine couldn't be convinced that it was for colored people too or that there would be any money left by the time she needed it. She was lighter-skinned than her daughter, like milk chocolate was to bittersweet, and so thin she could wrap her apron ties around her waist twice before tying them.

Mind you, Phoebe was just as loyal to Dellaphine as Dellaphine was to her. After Milton died under suspicious circumstances, the stock market took most of the Holcombe money and the Holcombe sons joined the military, the two women joined forces to open a boarding house. All of us knew Phoebe would brook no lack of respect toward Dellaphine, and since most boarding houses in Washington were crowded to the rafters and served no meals, even Henry Post, our crankiest boarder, learned to say please and thank you to Dellaphine.

'Let me take that,' Dellaphine said, reaching for my tray. 'You go on and see Miss Phoebe.'

I poked my head inside Phoebe's door.

Phoebe was sitting up in bed wrapped in a faded wool bathrobe, flipping through *Reader's Digest*. I often had to remind myself that Phoebe was only in her forties. Ada and I had talked her into growing her hair a bit and exchanging pin curls for finger waves but couldn't induce her to dye her greying hair. She still applied her lipstick so her mouth looked like a rosebud and wore cloche hats and skirts below her knees. It was as if she'd frozen in time in 1929, when the Depression hit and her husband died.

'How are you feeling?' I asked.

'Much better,' she said. 'I may live. How are things going in the house? I hate to leave Dellaphine with all this work.'

'We're fine,' I said. 'Milt made pancakes for breakfast and Henry even helped clean up while Dellaphine fixed the breakfast trays.'

Phoebe snorted. 'Henry? Cleaning up?'

'In a manly sort of way. He took out the trash.'

'What about Sunday dinner?'

'I'm going to help. It will be fine. Don't worry, just get well.'

Phoebe, her housekeeping worries relieved, leaned back against her pillows.

'So did you have fun last night?'

I remembered last night again. The freezing weather, the empty streets and the welcoming fire at the Baron Steuben Inn. Then the shocking discovery of a bloody corpse behind the bar. I wondered when Sergeant Royal was going to take my statement. I'd like to get it over with. I didn't see how Joe or I could contribute to the solution of the murder. Floyd Stinson had been dead for hours before we even entered the bar.

'Louise?'

'Oh, Phoebe, I'm sorry, my attention wandered.'

'I can see that. I was just wondering how *Madame Curie* was?'

'Marvelous,' I said. 'Greer Garson was just as good in it as the reviews said. It was worth about freezing to death to see.'

After I finished helping Dellaphine wash the Sunday dinner dishes and bring down Ada and Phoebe's lunch trays, I went into the lounge, where Henry and Milt were deep into the Sunday newspapers. Henry had the *Times-Herald*, of course; he hated Roosevelt almost as much as Cissy Patterson, the newspaper's editor, did. The rest of us were New Dealers and read the *Post*.

'Want the funnies?' Milt asked, holding the section out to me. He was handling the newspaper deftly, spreading it out over the coffee table so he could turn the pages one-handed.

He'd lost his left arm in the Pacific and had been discharged from the military.

'Please,' I said, taking the pages and settling into a chair next to the fire. The lounge window was patterned with a spider web of frost and the sky was iron grey. Once Ada and Phoebe were well we'd have to turn the heat down again, but until then we were cozy and warm. It seemed almost like a prewar winter Sunday, what with the Woodies ads advertising the usual Christmas gifts of wallets and perfume.

My mood plummeted when Milt passed me another section of the newspaper. The murder of a gangster, shown spread-eagled across a sidewalk near Union Station, headlined the crime section. As I had expected, there was no mention of the corpse behind the bar of the Baron Steuben Inn, but I was sure that, lurid and bloody as Floyd Stinson's murder was, it would dominate the page tomorrow. I wondered how well Sergeant Royal was doing with his interviews and what, if anything, he'd discovered at the crime scene today. I checked my watch. I hoped Royal would come take my statement today. I thought he would, if he wanted to finish his interviews before tomorrow. I wanted to get our meeting over with. For a second I had an urge to call Joe and ask if he'd spoken to Royal today. But the telephone in the hall was the only one in the house and I didn't want Milt and Henry to overhear me.

'Some coffee would taste good right now,' Henry said. He looked at me pointedly. I pretended not to notice. Just because I was the only girl in the room didn't mean it was my job to jump up and fix coffee.

'I'm going to ask Dellaphine to fix us some,' he said, moving to get up.

Milt looked up from the classified ads. 'Dellaphine has Sunday afternoon off, you know that,' he said. 'And she's been taking care of Mother and Ada.'

'That daughter of hers could help around here more,' Henry said.

'Madeleine doesn't work here,' I said, as calmly as I could. 'She has a regular job just like you do. She just lives here. Besides, she does help out.'

'I'll make us some coffee,' Milt said, rising to his feet. 'I need to learn how to do these things.' He left the room. Henry went back to his newspaper while I concentrated on not saying something rude to him.

The telephone in the hall rang. Milt answered it.

'Louise,' he called out. 'It's for you.'

Maybe it was Sergeant Royal. But when I picked up the receiver I heard the voice of Miss Alice Osborne, my boss at the Morale Operations branch of the Office of Strategic Services.

'Louise?' she said. What was this about?

'Yes, ma'am,' I answered.

'When you come to work tomorrow bring an overnight bag. We may need to spend a night or two here in the office.'

'Of course,' I said. Neither of us spoke another word. Our work was Top Secret. And that wasn't just a couple of words stamped on a few file folders. Even other branches of OSS, or army and navy intelligence, didn't know what we did. The Morale Operations unit produced 'black propaganda' designed to damage the morale of the enemy. We lied, essentially. We considered an operation a huge success when it was published in Allied newspapers as if it was the truth. Any leak could ruin weeks of work. I wondered if there was some kind of crisis at hand, or if the branch was just so short-staffed we needed to spend twenty-four hours a day there to get everything done. Miss Osborne and I couldn't discuss anything over the public telephone line. I'd just have to wait until tomorrow to find out.

THREE

Sergeant Harvey Royal limped into the Baron Steuben Inn and dropped heavily into a chair. He edged out of his coat and scarf and pulled off his gloves. This was a hell of a way to spend a cold Sunday morning. At his age he should be drinking coffee and listening to the Redskins game, looking forward to Sunday dinner at his niece's home.

'Dickenson, do you have my notebook?' he asked, rubbing his hands to warm them up.

His assistant handed him his notebook and pencil. Royal took them from him and flipped the book open. He looked around the room. The crime scene team was wrapping up. A dozen spent flashbulbs were scattered on the floor. Royal spotted the police photographer packing up his gear. 'You,' he said, 'pick up all these damn bulbs before you leave.'

'Yes, sir,' the photographer said.

'Is the doctor still here?' he asked a young policeman who was gingerly sorting through the detritus of an overturned trash can. A big one from behind the bar, judging from the empties lined up on the counter.

'He's in the bathroom washing up,' the policeman said.

'Get him for me, will you?' Royal asked Dickenson, who nodded and headed toward the back of the bar.

A police corporal almost as old as Royal but whose knees apparently still worked came over to him and tipped his cap.

'Sir,' he said, 'we're pretty much done here. Are you ready for a report?'

'Let me talk to the doctor first,' Royal said. He cast his eyes around the room.

'I don't suppose you've dusted for fingerprints.'

'Sir!' the corporal said. 'It's a bar! And not a clean one at that! There must be dozens of fingerprints on these surfaces!'

'So your answer is no,' Royal said.

'No,' the corporal said. 'I mean yes. I mean we didn't dust.'

'OK,' Royal said. Royal did everything by the book, but he had to agree that in this case fingerprints wouldn't narrow down suspects and would be useless to him.

The police doctor set his bag down on the table and eased into a chair next to Royal. His arthritis was almost as bad as Royal's, but he wasn't allowed to retire, either.

'So,' Royal said. 'Tell me.'

'You know nothing I say is engraved in stone until the autopsy,' the doctor said.

'Of course.'

'The victim died of multiple stab wounds. About six, I estimate, but I might find more once he's undressed and on the table. And I don't know what organs were damaged yet either, but it hardly matters since he lost enough blood to kill him, and quickly.'

'OK,' Royal said. 'Anything else? Time of death?'

'Yesterday, late afternoon. I'd guess he was in his forties and worked with his hands. His arm muscles were well developed and his hands were calloused. I saw no indication of other injuries or disease. Can I ship him to the morgue now?'

'Let me get a look at him first,' Royal said.

The sergeant pushed himself to his feet and with the help of his cane made his way behind the bar. The dead man lay in the same position as last night, stretched out with his hands placed neatly over his chest, like a body laid out for viewing.

'He didn't die here,' Royal said.

'No, sir,' the corporal said. 'He died in the storage room in back of the store. I'll show you.'

'In a minute,' Royal said.

The body was dressed in work boots, heavy canvas overalls and an antique flannel shirt. He wore suspenders but one had been sliced in two, probably by the murder weapon. A worn flat cap was pulled down over his forehead. A few strands of nondescript brown hair poked out around it.

'Have you found his overcoat?' Royal asked.

'No, sir,' the corporal said.

'He must have had an overcoat. No one would come out in this weather without one.'

'We're missing something else too.'

'What?'

'The murderer, or murderers, must have carried the victim from the storage room to here, but there's no blood on the barroom floor. He would have been bleeding like a stuck pig, so they would have had to wrap him in something. Whatever it was, we can't find it.'

'Maybe they wrapped him in his missing overcoat. Although I doubt that would be enough. You've looked out back in the garbage can?'

'Of course, sir,' the corporal said, miffed. 'And in every garbage can in the alley on this block. No overcoat, and nothing else he could have been wrapped in.'

'That would make a large bundle to dispose of,' Dickenson said.

'Yes, it would,' Royal said. He gestured to the doctor. 'You can take the body.

And you,' he said to the corporal, 'show me the murder scene.'

The small storage room at the back of the bar was obviously where Stinson had been killed. A dark pool of blood had soaked deep into its wood floors. Otherwise the room looked undisturbed. Shelves held tablecloths, neatly folded, glassware and cleaning supplies. A mop and bucket stood in the corner. Boxes of liquor and beer lined one wall.

'There's no sign of a struggle,' Dickenson said to Royal. 'Maybe the victim was unconscious.'

'Or the murderer straightened up afterwards,' the corporal said. He pointed to the stack of tablecloths. 'The body could have been wrapped up in one of those as well as the man's overcoat and then dragged behind the bar.'

'But why?' Dickenson said. 'Why move it? I'd think it was better hidden in here than outside under the bar.'

'Unless the barkeep was the murderer,' the corporal said. 'See, he didn't have time to dispose of the body before he had to open the bar. And he figured no one but him would be back there. Then after the bar closed he could get rid of it.'

Royal shook his head. 'I just don't see that kid – what's his name?'

'Calvin Doyle,' Dickenson answered.

'I just don't see him doing this. He's too scrawny to over-whelm Stinson, and if he took him by surprise I don't think he's strong enough to stab him that deep, either. Speaking of which, I'm sure you would have told me if you'd found the murder weapon,' Royal said to the corporal.

'The kid said he kept a nine-inch hunting knife in the store-room to slit open boxes and such. It's not there now. We've torn the place apart, searched the alley and emptied out all the trash cans on the block. We didn't find any knife, much less one that's large enough to inflict those wounds. There are some smaller knives behind the bar, the kind you slice lemons and limes with, but that's all.'

I resisted the impulse to help Milt. He was right, he needed to learn how to do things, and besides he looked like he had the coffee tray under control. Fortunately, if you could call it that, it was his left arm that he'd lost. Milt slid the tray on to the cocktail table. 'If you need anything else, you're going to have to get it yourself,' he said, glancing at Henry. He spoke lightly, but I knew Milt meant it.

'Is that teacake?' Henry said, placing his newspaper on the floor and reaching for the coffee pot. 'I thought we were running low on sugar.'

'Yeah,' Milt said, 'Dellaphine bought it at a bakery. It's a day old.'

Milt had brought a knife into the lounge to cut the cake with. It was Dellaphine's biggest kitchen knife, practically a cleaver, and when I picked it up I had a sudden vision of the dead man behind the bar at the Baron Steuben Inn. Including all the blood congealed on his clothing and the floor. I could swear I even smelled the metallic odor of the blood, but that couldn't be possible, could it? My hand tightened its grip on the knife handle. What would it be like to use a weapon like this against another person? I owned a Schrade switchblade, which had been issued to me during my training, and I'd used it once, but this knife was huge in comparison. It struck me that wielding it would require rage rather than skill. A rage I'd never experienced myself.

'Louise, what on earth?' Henry asked. His voice surprised me and I glanced up. He and Milt were staring at me.

'What are you thinking?' Milt asked. 'You've got quite a grip on that knife. It's just cake.'

'Oh,' I said, 'I'm sorry. I was distracted for a minute.' I took the tip of the knife and cut the cake into neat slices, then laid the knife down on the tray. I felt a sense of relief much greater than finishing such a small task warranted. As if I'd peered into the mind of a crazed murderer and then looked away again.

I wished that Sergeant Royal would interview me and get it over with. Maybe then I could forget what I'd seen.

Despite the cold a small crowd had gathered outside the Baron Steuben Inn to watch Stinson's body being loaded into the police mortuary van. When the van door slammed the crowd murmured as if they were one person, and began to disperse. Except for the reporters and photographers waiting to get inside.

'Vultures,' Dickenson said.

'They're just people,' Royal said. 'No better, no worse than most. They've got jobs to do.' He dropped his spent Camel on to the frozen sidewalk and crushed it with his shoe. 'Let's go talk to Cal Doyle now.' He glanced at the exterior staircase next to the bar that led upward to the second story. It was damned steep.

'Don't you want me to get him and bring him down to the bar?' Dickenson asked.

'No,' Royal said. 'I want to see him in his own place. I'll understand him better then. But I'll need a strong arm to help me get up there.'

'Done,' Dickenson said. With one arm over his assistant's shoulder and the other leaning on his cane, Royal made his way up the stairs. When he reached the landing he paused to lean on the banister and catch his breath.

They knocked on the only door at the head of the stairs and heard Calvin Doyle's voice say, 'Come in.'

The kid's room was small and sparse. A narrow bed piled with covers, a table with two mismatched chairs and a dresser with an electric ring and a pot encrusted with dried food about summed it up. The walls, though, were another story. They were plastered with pictures of pin-up girls torn from barbershop magazines. Cal appeared to prefer viewing the scenery from the rear. And airplanes, lots of airplane pictures, even a few fixed to the ceiling to look as if they were flying overhead.

Cal himself was tucked up in his bed wrapped in blankets holding a mug of cocoa.

In his pajamas he looked very young.

'How old are you?' Royal asked him.

'Twenty-three,' Cal answered.

'Sure,' Dickenson said.

'It's right there on my bartender's license, framed in the bar. I had to show them my birth certificate when I got it. I can't help that I look young.'

'You feeling any better today?' Royal asked him.

Cal shrugged, pulling his blanket around him. 'Yeah. The flu hit me hard. I got scarring in my lungs from pneumonia. That's why I ain't in the army. I tried to get into a training program to be an airplane mechanic but I flunked the entrance test.'

Dickenson grabbed the two chairs and plunked them down at Cal's bedside. He and Royal sat down and Royal pulled out his notebook.

'You won't need that,' Cal said to him. 'I ain't got nothing new to say.'

'Shut up and listen to the sergeant,' Dickenson said to him. 'Show some respect.' Royal laid his hand on his corporal's arm to silence him.

'It's for the record this time,' Royal said. 'Once it gets typed up you'll have to sign it, so it better be the truth.'

'I got nothing to hide,' the kid said.

'So tell it again, from the beginning,' Royal said.

'Like I said, I'd been sick, and I called my boss and told him I didn't want to work last night. He said he'd already lost too much money because the bar had been closed for two days and I had to open. I told him about my bad lung, and how most places was going to be closed because of the cold, and he told me if I didn't work he'd fire me. He's just looking for a reason to fire me, I think, because I get sick a lot. When I can't come in he has to tend the bar himself. I need this job, so I pulled myself together and called a taxi so I wouldn't have to walk over here and—'

'Wait a minute,' Royal said, looking up from his notebook. 'Where were you coming from? Weren't you here?'

'No,' Cal said. 'I was at my aunt's. Didn't I tell you that? She took care of me when I was sick on account of my bad lung.'

'So you weren't here in your room?'

'No,' Cal said. 'I told you. I was at my aunt's.'

'We need her address,' Dickenson said. Cal gave it to him.

'OK, go on,' Royal said.

'So I got here about six thirty so I could open on time at seven. When I went behind the bar I saw the dead guy. I recognized him, too, as the man who played chess with Mr Becker. I about had a heart attack, I'm telling you.'

'Did you touch him?' Dickenson asked.

'No, are you kidding? He was covered in blood.' Cal shuddered.

'So the way we saw him was the way you found him?' Royal asked.

'Yes, sir! I swear!'

'Then what happened?'

'I was scared. I didn't know what to do.'

'How about calling the police?' Dickenson asked.

'I wanted to talk to my boss first,' Cal said. 'I was already in trouble with him for being sick and missing work. You don't know him; he'd blame me for any bad publicity for the bar. But I couldn't. Right then some guys started knocking at the door. I'd turned on the neon martini glass already, you see. So I let them in. It was Walt and Chippy. They show up every Saturday as soon as we open. They drink beer until they run out of money.'

'So they're regulars,' Royal said.

'Yeah, so I couldn't call my boss then because the only telephone is the pay phone behind the bar. So I decided to wait until after we closed. Except then Walt came looking for whiskey and saw the corpse and you know what happened next. I ain't going through it again. It makes my breathing get all funny.'

'OK,' Royal said. 'Now tell me who came in next.'

'Huh?' Cal said.

'Who came into the bar after Walt and Chippy? Make sure you give me the names in the correct order.'

'OK. Well, Mr Becker with his chessboard. He took the seat by the fire. Then Miss Forrester, the woman with the book. She wanted coffee spiked with whiskey, but like I said we didn't have any, so she took brandy instead. Then those rich people. And then your friends.'

Royal listed their names in his notebook. Walt and Chippy, Al Becker, Mavis Forrester, Leo Maxwell and Gloria Scott, and Louise Pearlie and her friend, the foreign guy – Joe Prager, his name was. Royal disliked foreigners. He didn't like his country fighting their battles while these refugees, some of them rich royalty and the like, holed up here safe and sound. But if Prager was Louise's friend he was probably OK.

'What did your boss say when you told him what happened?' Dickenson asked.

'He said I done all right. And he seemed to think that having the bar in the news would bring customers, not scare them away.'

Royal and Dickenson smoked cigarettes in the car while they waited for the engine to warm up.

'Do you believe that kid's story?' Dickenson asked.

'You know, I do,' Royal said. 'Of course we need to confirm with his aunt. Besides, why would Cal kill the man? He was just a customer. What would he have to gain from it?'

'That kid's not running on all six,' Dickenson said. 'Imagine not having enough brains to call the police right away. It makes him look guilty as hell.'

'Just because he's stupid doesn't mean he's not telling the truth,' Royal said. Royal rarely felt sorry for anyone, including himself. Most people were the products of their own mistakes, he believed. But Royal pitied Cal. The kid probably never had more than a few bucks in his pocket and never would. He lived in one room, papered with pictures of women he'd never date and airplanes he'd never fix, from day to day hoping his lungs would keep working so he could hold down some kind of job. When the able-bodied men came back from the war he'd probably lose it. At least Royal had his pension coming.

The afternoon was interminable. I found my nerves stretched thin. I wondered why I had to get to work so quickly tomorrow and why I needed to bring a suitcase. Were we just short-staffed because of the flu, or had something happened in the war the public didn't know about yet? I worked in the European section of MO, so a crisis probably hadn't happened in the Pacific. In Europe anything could have happened – hell, Churchill might have died! There was a persistent rumor that he'd contracted pneumonia after getting back to England after the Tehran conference. I forced that thought from my mind. His death was unthinkable, I was being silly.

The whole country had a bad case of 'war nerves'. Tempers were short. It wasn't just whiskey that was scarce. So were Christmas gifts, especially children's toys, cosmetics, books and even gift-wrapping. I'd bought a fountain pen for Joe weeks ago, but everyone else on my list would have to be happy with gift certificates or war bonds.

There were shortages of everything from safety pins to flashlight batteries. Gas rationing had become a joke, for anyone who could afford to buy coupons or gas on the black market had all the gas they could want. Homes were freezing cold because Americans had followed the government's instructions and had converted from fuel oil to coal for heating, only to be confronted with coal shortages brought on by union strikes.

Adding to the general insecurity, President Roosevelt had been out of the country for over a month. We were a country without a leader; at least it felt like it. No president had ever been gone so long, much less in wartime, and in such exotic places.

Roosevelt had sailed to Dakar, then flown in a Douglas C-54 to Cairo and Tehran, then back to Cairo, then on to Carthage, Malta, Sicily, then back to Dakar. He'd first met up with Churchill and his entourage in Cairo to talk to the Turkish

Prime Minister, whom Stalin refused to invite to Tehran. Along
with most other Americans I had to look up Iran in the ency-
clopedia, where I learned that it was once Persia and was ruled
by a shah.

In Cairo Roosevelt had Thanksgiving dinner at the Mena
Hotel. According to *Time* magazine, while the Americans,
British and Turks discussed invasion strategy they'd consumed
22,000 pounds of meat, 1,000 pounds of coffee, 17,000 pounds
of bread, 78,000 eggs, 740 pounds of tea, 5,000 cans of milk,
800 pounds of turkey, 4,600 pounds of sugar, 19,000 pounds
of potatoes, 5,000 cans of fruit, 3,000 cigars and a million
cigarettes. Thus fortified, they'd flown on to Tehran, the capital
of Iran, to discuss the Second Front with Joseph Stalin at the
Russian embassy there.

The Russian army threw an armed perimeter around the
Russian and British embassies because German paratroopers
had landed in the vicinity and hadn't all been captured. Even
the janitors in the Russian embassy were armed.

It was public knowledge that the three leaders had discussed
an invasion of Europe. But that was all anyone knew.

The public didn't know this yet either, but I'd heard at work
that President Roosevelt had left Dakar on the USS *Iowa* three
days ago to head back to Washington. The country would
breathe a collective sigh of relief when he was back at the
White House.

Then there was the incident of the corpse in the bar, which
sounded like the title of an Agatha Christie novel. My OSS
training had kicked in and I'd dealt with it coolly, but now I
felt shaky. I just wanted to sign a statement and put it behind
me. I wondered if Joe had heard from Sergeant Royal yet today.

I was alone in the lounge. Henry and Milt had succumbed
to cabin fever and gone out for a walk in the freezing cold.
Ada and Phoebe were still in bed. Madeleine and Dellaphine
were in the kitchen. I could hear the gospel music from
Dellaphine's big Silvertone radio drifting down the hall.

I could call Joe. I slipped out into the hall and lifted the
telephone receiver.

'Hello,' he said, picking up the phone after two rings. 'This
is a pleasant surprise. Are you alone?'

'Sort of,' I whispered. 'There's no one around. I wondered if you'd heard from Sergeant Royal yet.'

'Not a word. But that makes sense, doesn't it? I mean, we were the last people who arrived at the bar, so he'd interview us last, wouldn't he?'

'I just want to get it over with,' I said.

'Me too. And no matter what Sergeant Royal says, I'll have to tell my bosses at work what happened tomorrow. Can't have them surprised by seeing my name in a crime news story.'

'I know.' I would need to tell Miss Osborne too.

I heard Milt and Henry's voices as they came up the walkway to the house.

'I've got to go now,' I said.

'Will I see you on the weekend?' he asked.

'Hope so.' I cradled the receiver. I had no idea if I'd be available to see Joe on the weekend. My work schedule wasn't my own. And was confidential to boot. But we were both used to that.

Milt and Henry brought winter into the house with them. When the door opened a gust of wind blew into the hall and pushed magazines off the hall table on to the floor. Milt had to lean into the door to latch it closed. Bits of ice, condensed from their breath, clung to their scarves. The air was so frigid it was scary. We were rationing coal just like everyone else, but at least we had it and were allowed to turn up the heat if there was sickness in the house. In Britain the people lived from one convoy fuel delivery to the next. They never had more than three months' supply on hand, and this winter and the flu epidemic was harsher there than here. Honestly, I had no idea how the British people got through their days. I suppose they had no choice.

Milt slid out of his heavy coat, shaking his head at Henry when he tried to help him. With one hand he got it off and hung it on the coatrack.

'Who was on the phone?' Henry asked me.

'Wrong number,' I said.

FOUR

Mavis Forrester opened her apartment door after the first knock.

'Come in,' she said. 'I've been expecting you.'

'Thanks,' Royal said, as he and Dickenson shed their coats, scarves and gloves.

'Just toss them on the table,' Mavis said. She was dressed in what Royal thought would be called lounging pajamas in a Hecht's ad. Black satin trousers matched a floral jacket with the same black satin trim. She wore embroidered slippers and a heavy shawl thrown over it all for warmth.

'Sit,' Mavis said, gesturing toward an overstuffed loveseat. She sat down on a matching chair and crossed her legs. She had a cup of something hot, coffee or tea, on a table next to her but didn't offer them anything. *The Robe* lay open next to her cup.

Royal saw no signs that the woman had a roommate. 'You live here alone?' he asked.

'Not that it's any of your business,' she said, 'but yes.'

'It is our business, ma'am,' Royal answered. 'In case we need to verify elements of your story.'

Mavis shrugged. 'Sorry,' she said. 'I live alone, happily.'

It was a one-bedroom, too, Royal thought, not a studio, noting the door to the bedroom and another to a small kitchen. Her furniture was quality, and a couple of small paintings hanging on the wall looked like real art. He wondered how much money librarians made and if the DC Housing Authority knew she occupied a two-room apartment by herself.

'OK,' Royal said. 'When did you arrive at the bar?'

'About eight,' she said.

'Why did you even go? In that weather?'

'I wanted a cup of hot coffee, spiked, in the worst way. I was out of whiskey and can't buy another bottle until tomorrow.

And I knew the fire would be blazing. I love a good fire. So I wrapped up and took a book with me to read for a while.'

'So who was there when you arrived?"

'The usuals. Walt, Chippy and Al. On Saturday night they are almost always there. Of course last night Floyd never arrived to play chess with Al.'

'Did he seem surprised?'

'Al? Yes. He kept checking his watch, and once he asked Cal if he'd heard from Floyd that day, or seen him. Cal said no.'

'You must be a regular at the Baron Steuben.'

Mavis shrugged. 'Not really. I mean, it's the closest bar to my apartment. So when I do want a drink, I go there. It's the fire I like, especially in this weather. If I want a drink I can have one here. As long as I've got a bottle of whiskey, that is.'

'You don't meet friends there?' Dickenson asked.

'I don't socialize in bars, Sergeant.' Mavis said. 'I go to nice restaurants or the theater with my friends.'

'Who came in next?'

'Maxwell and Scott. The rich couple. Then that other woman and her friend, I've forgotten their names.'

'Louise Pearlie and Joe Prager.'

'If you say so.'

'Ever seen either couple in the bar before?'

'Never.'

'All right,' Royal said. 'So tell us what happened, in your own words.'

'Is that really necessary?' she asked. 'I thought Mrs Pearlie did a good job telling what happened last night.'

'Yes, it's necessary.'

Royal and Dickenson waited patiently for her to light a cigarette. She refused Dickenson's offer to light it for her. Again she didn't offer them one, or invite them to smoke their own. When she spoke it was with such diffidence that she could have been talking about a traffic violation. Her account of Walt's finding Stinson's corpse and its aftermath didn't differ one iota from any of the other statements they'd taken.

'Thank you, ma'am,' Royal said, shutting his notebook.

'We'll get this typed up and a policeman will bring it by for you to sign.'

'OK,' she said. She crushed her cigarette and walked them to her door. As it closed Royal saw her cross to her chair, hand reaching for her book.

'Man,' Dickinson said as he opened the police car for Royal. 'That woman is an icicle.' He crossed around to the driver's side and slid in, turning on the ignition to warm up the car.

'A real cold fish,' Royal agreed. 'I wonder what she's been through in her life to make her that way.'

I had my late husband's battered leather valise open on my bed, trying to decide what to take to the office tomorrow so I could spend the night. I had seen a cot with blankets and a pillow in Miss Osborne's office the first day I arrived at the Morale Operations branch to take up my new job as her assistant, so I knew overnight stays were likely. So was traveling. In the fall I'd taken my first airplane flight and found myself on the Fort Meade military base interviewing German prisoners of war. Anything was possible. Which was why I loved my new job.

I assumed the branch would provide cots, blankets and pillows. Lots of blankets, I hoped, especially in this weather. MO was located in the Que building on the OSS campus, a tempo built so poorly I was surprised it hadn't blown over in this wind. Those of us who worked there had spent what free time we had chinking the gaps in the exterior walls with whatever we could find. Discarded paper, rags and even used chewing gum spotted the walls of our tiny spaces.

I decided to wear as many clothes as I could to work tomorrow and fill my valise with extras. I'd start with my grey wool suit, the one with green piping, worn over two sweaters, a white turtleneck and a green cardigan. I'd drape a long shawl that Phoebe had given me over my wool coat. Hat and gloves, of course. Ear muffs. Forget heels and stockings, I'd wear saddle shoes and socks. Into my valise I put my long underwear and a pair of corduroy trousers. As many heavy socks as I could stuff into the corners. Several pairs of fresh undies; I could always wash those out. No pajamas, because of course I would sleep in my clothes. Both because of the weather and because there would be men spending the night too, I expected.

I was stuffing cold cream, tooth powder and aspirin into my toilet bag when Phoebe passed by my open bedroom door.

'Hi, there,' I said to her. 'You must be feeling better.'

'I am, thanks,' she said. 'Much. I'm going downstairs to fix myself some hot chocolate. I don't want Dellaphine to have to run up and down the stairs again.' She spied the piles of clothing on my bed.

'What on earth?' she said. 'Looks like you're going on an expedition to the North Pole.'

'Almost,' I said. 'My boss told me to come to work prepared to spend the night in the office tomorrow. Maybe more than one night.'

'Oh, Louise,' she said, leaning up against my doorjamb as if she'd lost all her strength.

'What's wrong, Phoebe?' I asked, worried. 'Maybe you should get back to bed. I'll go get your hot chocolate.'

Instead, Phoebe came inside my room and turned and gently closed my door.

'What is it?' I asked. 'Is something wrong?'

'Dearie,' she said, 'I am so worried about you.'

'Why? I'm fine.'

Phoebe pushed aside the piles of clothes I'd stacked on my bed ready to pack and sat down.

'You just can't do this,' she said.

'Do what?' I was mystified. What was Phoebe talking about?

'Go gadding about the way you have recently. It was bad enough when you were gone before. A young lady like yourself spending weeks at a military base! What would your parents think?'

So that was it. Phoebe was concerned about my reputation. I almost snapped at her. I was thirty years old, a widow, and I had a critically important government job. Besides, I'd been quartered in a WAC dormitory with my female boss and we worked almost constantly. Of course I couldn't share anything with her about my job. Even the smallest details were confidential. All Phoebe knew for sure was that I took off by myself with a suitcase and said it was on business. Something that in her day would have been unheard of.

But the tears in her eyes softened my response, and I wanted to reassure her. She wouldn't be so upset if she weren't fond of me.

I sat down next to her on the bed and took her hand. 'Phoebe, I promise you there's nothing disreputable about this. It's just a government office. The flu has caused so many absences, work is piling up, and late at night it's dangerous to try to get home in this weather. So many of the buses and streetcars aren't running. It's safer to sleep at work, really. There will be lots of other people bunking down at the office, too. I'll be perfectly safe and well chaperoned.' I winced at that word. As if a woman my age should need a chaperone!

'It's just that I don't want you to get a reputation like Ada's,' she said. 'All that partying, drinking, staying out so late. The men who pick her up at those dances she plays at, their intentions are indecent.' Ada's intentions weren't decent, either. She constantly sought distraction from the secret of her marriage to a German Luftwaffe pilot, something only I knew about. She'd married him before the war, of course, before he'd become converted to the Nazi Party. Drinking and partying was her way of avoiding her great fear: that someone, somehow, would find out that she was married to a Nazi.

'I won't get a reputation like Ada's from doing my job,' I said.

'You could get a different job,' she said. 'One where you can keep respectable hours.'

Filing and typing, I thought. I'd had enough of that.

'I just want you to find a nice man,' Phoebe said, wiping her eyes on the corner of her robe. 'Someone who can take care of you.'

'I'm not looking for another husband. I can take care of myself.'

'Dearie, after the war is over all these jobs that women are doing now will be gone. What will you do then if you haven't remarried?'

I felt my stomach knot. She'd touched a sensitive spot. All

of us government girls had been hired 'for the duration'. What would I do after the war? I could no longer imagine living without my own paycheck.

I patted Phoebe on the hand. 'Stop worrying about me,' I said. 'I'm fine, really. You've got enough to do worrying about Milt and Tom and taking care of the rest of us. I promise my behavior is beyond reproach.'

At that Phoebe smiled at me, and patted my hand in return. 'All right,' she said. 'If you say so. I'll leave you be and let you finish packing.'

After I closed the door behind her my stomach cramped so severely it doubled me up for a second. I had to sit on my bed and collect myself.

The problem was, my behavior wasn't beyond reproach. I was shacked up with Joe Prager, a man I knew very little about, a Czech refugee who ostensibly taught Slavic languages at George Washington University, but whose real work was undercover at a Jewish charitable organization raising money to rescue Jews from Europe. He'd been Henry's roommate until Milt returned from the Pacific theater. We'd been attracted to each other from the moment we met, and now spent long weekend afternoons alone together in a single bed in Joe's apartment.

Although wartime Washington, DC had become positively worldly, my behavior would still shock most people. Including Phoebe, obviously. No matter how fond she was of me she might very well evict me if she knew Joe and I were more than friends. And the repercussions of my dalliance might lose me my job, too. I had Top Secret clearance, which could be revoked if OSS knew I was intimate with a foreign refugee. I'd be out of work and out of a place to live. Back deep-frying hush puppies at my parents' fish camp in Wilmington, North Carolina. I'd have to give up martinis, my Woodies charge account and my dream of owning my own car.

That was why Joe and I were so careful. If we ran into someone I knew from the office I could never pass him off as just a casual date. His accent would take care of that.

Clearly we needed to be even more careful about being seen in public.

Then I remembered the adverse possibilities of the incident at the Baron Steuben Inn. If my name, and Joe's, appeared in the paper it would be publicity OSS and Miss Osborne wouldn't appreciate, even if it weren't my doing. I needed to tell her what had happened first thing tomorrow morning.

The newspapers would undoubtedly sensationalize Stinson's murder. I could just see the headlines. 'Body Lies under Bar while Customers Drink Cocktails' was just one phrase I could imagine. My name would be listed on the police blotter as a witness. The question was, would the reporters bother to mention me by name? I wished Sergeant Royal would come on and interview me and get it over with.

It was a good thing the police got extra gasoline rations, Royal thought as Dickenson drove him north, on across the Taft Bridge which carried Connecticut Avenue over the Rock Creek Gorge. Of course, Becker worked at the zoo, which was sited in Rock Creek Park north of the bridge, so it was close to his work. His building, the Woodward Apartments, was a handsome one right across the street from the Wardman Park Hotel, where so many new Washingtonians lived, either in the hotel itself or in the apartments behind it. Dickenson parked and then followed Royal as he made his way up the steps to the building's double door. Before the war he would have waited for a doorman to answer a doorbell ring, but there weren't many doormen anymore. He simply pushed the door open and went inside. The small, dark lobby was paved with marble black-and-white squares. A couple of veined black marble columns reached from the floor to the ceiling. No one sat at the desk near the entrance. Dickenson swung the elevator door and cage door open and they went inside the elevator, which was paneled in bright brass. No elevator operator, either. Royal pushed the button for the third floor.

Al Becker opened the door to his apartment and ushered Royal and Dickenson inside. A davenport covered in mauve velveteen with two matching chairs filled the half of the room near the windows while a small dining area occupied the other half. Two bookshelves crammed with books and fronted by a

Philco console radio lined the longest wall. An arch opened into a small but modern kitchen.

Al moved sections of the *Washington Post* off the davenport and tossed them on the dining table. 'Please have a seat,' he said, and then moved to the radio to turn off the news. 'Would you like some coffee? I can make a fresh pot.'

'No thanks,' Royal said, pulling out his notebook. 'This is a nice apartment, nice building.'

'Thank you,' Al said. 'My wife and I moved here after I began working at the zoo. We had a two-bedroom apartment first, but then after my daughter left home and my wife died, well, one bedroom is enough for me. And of course the city needed two-bedrooms for government workers.'

'You are German?' Royal asked.

'You don't waste time, Sergeant, asking the obvious question. I'm an American citizen, but yes, I am originally from Germany.'

'When did you say you arrived here?' Royal asked.

'What does this have to do with Floyd's murder?'

'Please answer my questions, Mr Becker.'

'I immigrated here after the First World War,' Al said. 'My wife was an American, so when we married I became a citizen.'

'What did you do for a living? Did you speak English then?'

'I was a bicycle messenger,' Al said. 'I had strong legs. I took English in a class at the Post Office. With my wife's help I became fluent quickly and finished a clerical course. I went to work at the zoo in administration in 1933.'

'Mr Becker,' Dickenson said, 'would you mind if I used your bathroom?'

Al turned to him. 'Officer,' he said, 'if you want to look around my apartment, go right ahead. You won't see any swastikas or pictures of Hitler.'

Royal nodded at Dickenson, who got up and went back toward the bedroom and bathroom.

'Do you mind if I smoke?' Royal asked Al.

'Not at all,' Al said, getting up to fetch an ashtray.

Royal took his time tapping a cigarette out of a pack of Camels and lighting it, giving Al time to compose himself.

'I don't mean to insult you, Mr Becker,' he said. 'But the murder victim was an acquaintance of yours, and you were in the bar when his body was discovered.'

The flush of anger faded from Al's cheeks. 'I understand. It is hard to be of German birth these days. None of my neighbors speak to me anymore, even though we were friends before the war.'

'You told me that you didn't know Floyd Stinson well?'

'That's correct. I met him in the bar.'

'Why go so far from your neighborhood?'

'The Baron Steuben used to stock a large selection of German beers. It's close to the old German embassy, you know. And my wife and I attended the Lutheran church around the corner. I enjoyed going there and speaking my native language. When Hitler came to power I stopped, I couldn't bear the Nazi uniforms and flags. But after the embassy closed I began to return again. I hoped to run into old friends, but I didn't. Everything has changed so much. But I did meet Floyd, and since he lived nearby and didn't have a car, I continued to go to the Baron Steuben for our chess games.'

'I find it hard to believe you didn't know what he did for a living,' Royal said.

Al shrugged. 'I didn't think much of it. I figured he had a government job in some office. That's why I was so surprised to see him in work clothes when I saw his body.'

'Did you ever see him outside of playing chess?'

'Sometimes we had dinner first at a café down the street. But it was closed yesterday because of the weather.'

Dickenson came back into the living room. 'The place is clean, sir,' he said.

'Tell me, Sergeant, have you searched the homes of the other people who were in the bar?' Al asked. 'Or did you do that just because I was born in Germany?'

'Yeah, because you're German,' Royal said. 'Get over it. We're at war.'

I was intensely relieved to open the door and find Sergeant Royal on my doorstep. Officer Dickenson wasn't with him.

'Please come in,' I said. 'I'm glad to see you. I thought maybe you wouldn't make it today.'

Royal limped inside and shed his outer clothing. I hung it on the crowded coatrack. 'Where's your sidekick?' I asked him.

'Sent him on an errand so you and I could have a friendly conversation,' Royal said. 'I don't want him to know that you and I are friends, and that you helped me work a murder case a while back. Figured you didn't want him to know, either.'

I certainly didn't. And neither did OSS.

'We're low on coffee,' I said. 'Can I get you something else? Tea? Hot chocolate?'

'Now that hot chocolate sounds good,' Royal said. 'I haven't had any in years.'

I showed Royal into the lounge and went back to the kitchen. Heating milk until just a few bubbles showed around the edge of the pot, I stirred in cocoa and sugar until the granules dissolved. When I took the mug into the lounge Royal had made himself comfortable, propping one leg on the cocktail table.

'I can tell how much your knees hurt,' I said. 'I thought you were going to retire by now? Can't you have anything for the pain?'

'I can't take laudanum during the day. It affects me, makes it hard to concentrate. What I need is to quit and get off my feet. But I reckon I'm going to have to work until the end of the war. Dickenson is a help.'

He sipped on the steaming chocolate. 'Man, that's good,' he said. 'Brings back memories. So tell me why you're so glad to see me.'

'You know I'll have to inform my superiors about the murder,' I said. 'But then you'd said not to mention this at work until we talked. I couldn't do that. If my boss sees my name in the newspapers as a witness in a murder investigation and I haven't told her I'll be out of my job. And I like working.'

'Her? Your boss is a woman?'

I didn't answer him directly. 'I have a new position. It's more confidential than the last one.'

'Good,' Royal said, finishing his cocoa. 'You were wasted as a file clerk.'

'Thanks,' I said.

'No details of your new duties are available?' he asked.

'Nope.'

'Police work was hard enough before the war, before everyone in this town had some vital secret to keep,' he said. He pulled out his notebook. 'Look, I'm going to read the statement you made last night. If it's OK I'll get it typed up as it is. There's no reason for you to tell me the whole story again.'

He read it to me, almost word for word what I had said last night.

'It's fine,' I said.

Royal stuck the notebook back in his pocket.

'Are you done with your interviews now?' I asked.

'Are your fellow boarders apt to walk in?'

I shook my head. 'No. Ada and Phoebe are in bed resting. Dellaphine and Madeleine are downstairs in their room. Milt and Henry are upstairs in theirs. Since we have flu in the house we're allowed to keep the heat turned up, and everyone is using that time to be by themselves instead of crammed together down here in front of the fireplace or in the kitchen.'

'Considering your security clearance I don't mind telling you that I talked to your friend Joe Prager before I came here. Of course he verified everything you said. He seemed OK for a foreigner.'

I felt myself bristle. 'What's that got to do with anything?'

'It seems like half the people in this town got here after 1938, too many of them from other countries. How can I check on their backgrounds? How do I know if they are who they say they are? I don't. Your friend could be a renowned European jewel thief using a forged passport.'

I couldn't help but smile when I pictured Joe dressed in black scaling the rooftops of Paris or Monaco.

'Don't laugh, it's not funny.'

'Not to you, maybe. So what can you tell me?'

'The first thing Dickenson and I did this morning was interview Cal. He stuck to that loony story of his, that he found the body behind the bar and decided not to do anything about it until closing time! But he's just brainless enough, and scared enough, to do it.'

'He was so terrified the entire time we were in the bar, we thought he was deathly ill.'

'He's not healthy, that's clear. I doubt he's strong enough to have done the deed. Which doesn't mean he's not involved, of course. And as Dickenson and I left the crime scene, newspaper reporters and photographers were hovering like vultures around the bar, just waiting for the scene to be released so they could take their grisly photographs. I'm sure they've found Cal too by now and pumped him for details. Too late for today's paper; it will all be laid out in tomorrow's.'

'I'm praying they leave my name out of their stories,' I said.

Royal shrugged. 'With luck they'll be more interested in the victim and the society parasites who slipped out the back door than in you. Speaking of whom, I couldn't talk to the lovebirds today. I didn't make it past the butler at the Maxwell pile. It's just a few mansions down from the Baron Steuben on the other side of Massachusetts, the fancy side. The butler said Maxwell wasn't in, and I couldn't prove he was. I'll get to him eventually. And we can't locate Mrs Scott. She's checked out of her hotel. Avoiding the press, I guess. We'll run her to ground too, though. Then we went to see Mavis Forrester. She had nothing new to add to your story, either. That broad is tough, I am telling you.'

'She was reading her book the entire time we were waiting for the police. She didn't seem more than irritated that there was a body behind the bar.' The phrase still sounded like the title of an Agatha Christie whodunit to me. 'Did you notice her mink coat?'

'Yeah, takes a lot of pocket lettuce to buy one of those. You wouldn't expect her to be alone. Without a man, I mean. And Al Becker puzzles me. I can't quite believe that he didn't know any more about Stinson than he said he did. If they played chess every week, what did they talk about? And he has a chip on his shoulder. Says that people distrust him because he's German.'

'I don't blame him,' I said. 'He's an American. Has been

for years now. It must be awful for people to dislike him just because he has a German accent.'

'What does he expect? We're in the middle of a world war started by Germany. It's not my job to be considerate and understanding. It's my job to find out who killed Floyd Stinson.'

Royal finished his cocoa and set the mug down on the coffee table. He stretched his leg, moving it from the coffee table to the floor, wincing.

'Then I went on to talk to Walt,' he continued. 'He was just what I expected. Low on amps and voltage. Lives in a two-bedroom apartment with his wife and kids. He's driven the same bus route up and down Massachusetts Avenue for years. He told me that he'd seen Al, Floyd and Mavis on his bus before, many times. Every Saturday night he meets his friend Chippy at the Baron Steuben for sandwiches and beer. Then I moved on to Chippy. He's a loser who lives in a dingy room in an alley boarding house. Since he's a jailbird the only work he could find was as a pinsetter in a bowling alley, a colored boy's job. He ran off from the bar because he didn't want anything to do with the police. I'm inclined to think neither he nor Walt is involved in the murder.'

'So what you're telling me, Officer Royal, is that you've got nothing,' I said to him, grinning.

'Not yet. But I'll find out who killed Floyd Stinson. Police work is more about persistence than anything else. Stubbornness is my finest attribute. There's one thing that's really unusual about this case, though.'

'What?'

'No one seems to know anything about the victim. Even though he's been playing chess with Al for months, and frequented the bar before that, the other regulars didn't know where he lived or worked. We'll take his fingerprints at the morgue, of course, and ask the FBI to run them. Then we'll know more about him than his mother does.'

The FBI. The last people in Washington I wanted to have anything to do with – any more than I already had, that was.

'At least you have a good timeline of events at the bar to work with,' I said.

Royal grinned at me. 'You think so?'

'Don't you?'

He shook his head. 'Louise,' he said, 'I believe you told me the truth. As to what happened before you and your friend Mr Prager walked into the bar, I don't know for sure, and neither do you. Everyone else there could be lying in their teeth.'

FIVE

I slipped quietly downstairs and looked for the *Washington Post*. Dellaphine had brought it in, but it lay untouched on the cocktail table in the lounge. I grabbed it up and leafed through until I reached the crime section. 'Body behind a Bar, while Customers Drank', the headline blared. My stomach clutched again. The subheadings read 'Maxwell Heir and Gloria Scott Flee' and 'Bartender Tells Gruesome Tale'. A photograph focusing on the interior of the Baron Steuben Inn, plus an old photo of Maxwell and Scott, completed the visual side of the story. I skimmed the article and didn't find my name, or Joe's. Or Walt's, Chippy's or Al's. We were just 'other witnesses'. Cal was the star of the piece. He talked his head off to the reporter, including all the gory details. I was ready to bet that bar would be packed tonight, despite the persistent cold weather. Cal could hold forth to the customers and collect some good tips. His boss would be happy and wouldn't fire him.

After catching my breath I reread the article more carefully. My name was still not there, thank God. That was something positive I could tell Miss Osborne. I folded the paper just as Milt came into the room

'You're up early,' he said. Then he spied the luggage I'd brought downstairs with me.

'Going somewhere?' he asked.

'Work,' I said. 'I may be gone for a couple of nights.'

'Mother won't approve,' he said. He sat on the davenport and shook out the paper with one hand, opening it to the classified ads.

'I know. She's already told me,' I said.

'Don't worry about it. The world has changed, and she'll have to accept it someday. God knows,' he said, looking at his empty sleeve, 'it's changed for me.' He flipped a page.

'Looking for a new job?' I asked.

'Yeah. I just can't see myself as an elevator operator for the rest of my life, even if it only takes one arm.'

The unmarked black Chevy coupe pulled up to the curb. I spotted it through the window; it was too gusty outside to wait on the sidewalk. I grabbed my valise and dashed out. The driver didn't get out to open the door for me, and I didn't blame him. I opened the back door myself, hearing the lock crackle as the ice inside shattered, and flung my valise into the back seat, sliding in after it. The car heater was blasting, thank goodness.

It wasn't far to the OSS compound. Traffic was light, since so many people were either home sick or told to stay away from work. The Chevy pulled up at the back gate of the compound. This time the driver opened the door for me. I toted my valise to the gate, where the guard, who was wearing an army parka trimmed with fur, nodded me through when he saw my OSS badge.

Que building was at the southwest corner of the OSS complex, a walled compound tucked between 'E' Street and Constitution. The Potomac River and the Water Gate were just a couple of blocks to the west where Rock Creek Parkway followed the river. The War Department was two blocks away from the compound to the east. If you walked five more blocks to the east you'd run into the State Department and then into the White House.

An army infantry company guarded both OSS and the War Department.

Other buildings in the complex included the Old Naval Hospital, where General Donovan and the other OSS big shots had their offices. OSS staff liked to call it 'the Kremlin' when they were sure no one important could overhear them. Other buildings housed diverse OSS units like Procurement, Medical Services, Schools and Training, and Motor Transport. The Deputy Director of Intelligence John Magruder and his staff took up most of Central Building, which also housed the Planning Committee. One of the duties of the Planning Committee was to approve the psychological warfare operations proposed by my branch, Morale Operations. The South Building, the largest building on the campus, held Communications,

Special Funds, the Naval Command, Security and the Research and Development branch. My earlier job, at the Registry, had been outside the compound at Annex #1, an old apartment house. I was thrilled to be located now where the action was, so to speak.

The complex, usually bustling, seemed almost deserted except for our army guards, all wearing arctic gear like the guard at the gate. A few staff hurried from building to building, heads down against the chilly gusts of wind. Once inside Que I found the building even quieter than I had expected. The artists' workroom, usually a beehive of activity, held only a couple of people, one adding color to an anti-Nazi poster and another painstakingly inking in antique German letters on a pamphlet layout. A portable electric heater warmed the space so the artists could work without their coats.

I pulled off my gloves and hat.

'This is bad,' I said. The colorist pulled off her fingerless gloves and rubbed her hands together. 'Most of the branch is out,' she said. 'Everyone came down with the flu at once.'

'It's that damn cafeteria,' the calligrapher said. 'Crowded with people and their germs. If you don't want to get sick you should bring your own lunch,' he said, lifting a brown paper bag from the desk in front of him.

Both had suitcases standing next to their chairs, so I wasn't the only one prepared to spend the night.

I edged open my office door. I still couldn't get over having a workspace of my own, despite how tiny and dark it was. The typewriter, the crowded inboxes and outboxes, the office supplies, even the dreaded file cabinet, all belonged to me alone. Even better, I could work without wrapping my fingers in bandages to protect them from paper cuts or fending off other people's elbows in the narrow aisles between the rows of files in the Registry. I didn't see a cot set up in my office yet; surely I wouldn't need to sleep on the floor. Someone must be bringing me one later.

Miss Osborne, the Assistant Director of European Theater for MO and my boss, poked her head in my door. If I hadn't been wrapped in so many layers myself I would have laughed. She wore corduroy trousers with long johns poking out at the ankles, a man's pullover wool sweater that hung down to her knees and an *ushanka* with the earflaps down.

'Louise,' she said, 'good morning. Good to see you. Don't get settled. Leave your valise here for now, grab your typewriter and some office supplies. You and I are working in the conference room. Office Services set up a coal tent stove in there. It's positively cozy. We, the women, that is, are going to sleep in there tonight.'

'That's quite a hat,' I said, grinning. 'You look like a Russian reindeer herder.'

Miss Osborne patted her *ushanka*. It was made of sheepskin, with the skin on the outside and the wool lining the inside. It was too big for her and settled on her head just above her glasses, even with the forehead flap tied up. The earflaps tied snugly under her chin.

'You're just jealous,' she said. 'My father brought this back after the First World War. He was part of the American Expeditionary Force in Siberia. He claimed this hat was the only reason he got back to the States with both ears still attached to his head.'

'Wait, Miss Osborne,' I said, as she turned to leave the room. 'I have to tell you something terribly important.'

'Tell me in the conference room, why don't you; we can get coffee on the way.'

'I'd rather do it here, where I know we can talk in private,' I said.

She raised an eyebrow, then sat on the corner of my desk. 'Spit it out.'

'Have you read the *Post* this morning?'

'I read it cover to cover every morning, you know that.'

'Did you see the article about the corpse in the Baron Steuben Inn?'

'The one where a murder victim was hidden behind a bar while there were customers on the premises? I sure did. What a story. And the Maxwell heir was there with his current inamorata. That should keep the gossip columnists busy.'

'I was there too,' I said.

'What! Oh, Louise, no you weren't!'

'I was with my friend Joe Prager.'

'Joe Prager? Do I know him?' I explained that Joe was my Czech friend who was able to help us answer some questions we had about a German–Czech town when we were interviewing German prisoners of war a few months ago.

'Joe has a British passport and a job here. He teaches Slavic languages at George Washington University. He used to room at my boarding house.'

'You know how OSS Security hates publicity of any kind.'

'Yes, ma'am, but the article didn't mention my name. The press was more interested in Maxwell and his girlfriend. And the barkeep.'

'Tell me the whole story.'

I told her everything.

She chewed on her pencil for a minute. 'You were interviewed by the police, of course.'

That was when I told her that I knew Sergeant Royal very well.

'He doesn't know that you work for OSS!'

I felt my neck begin to knot and pain threaten my temples.

Seeing my expression, Miss Osborne leaped to her feet.

'Louise! No!'

'I assisted him when he investigated the death of an OSS staffer. Remember the man who drowned in the tidal pool? You must have read about it in my file.'

'Oh,' she said, subsiding, 'that. Well, you haven't done anything wrong. You were just in the wrong place at the wrong time. Do you think this Sergeant Royal will keep you out of this?'

'He'll do his best,' I said. 'We became quite good friends. There were plenty of other witnesses. Joe and I were the last people to come into the bar before the body was discovered, so I don't think we've got any unique information.'

'OK. Just keep me informed. Anything I need to pass on to Security, let me know.'

'Yes, ma'am,' I said.

'And this Joe person,' she said. 'You know Security doesn't like our personnel fraternizing with refugees, even if they are respectable.'

'He's just a friend.'

'Don't attract attention to yourselves.' She stood up and adjusted her heavy sweater. 'Let's get on to the conference room.'

At least she hadn't told me to cut off Joe, I thought, as I followed her down the hall. I didn't know what I'd do if I ever got a direct order not to see him. The thought made my stomach knot into a painful ball that felt like I'd swallowed a walnut whole.

We stopped at the coffee table and filled our cups on the way to the conference room. As Miss Osborne stirred her milk into her coffee she smiled at me in an odd way, as if she was keeping a secret from me.

'What is it?' I asked.

'Let's just say you're going to be surprised when you meet the person we're conferring with this morning. Pleasantly surprised.'

Merle was already in the conference room with another man, a civilian sitting with his legs crossed, reading the contents of a thick folder. He was an ordinary-looking person, perhaps better dressed than the average bureaucrat, except for the odd impression he gave because his hair was dark and slicked back but his beard was white and curly. He looked up from his work when Miss Osborne and I entered and stood up. My mouth went dry when I saw his face full on. It was Rex Stout! One of my favorite authors. I consumed his books like Milt went through a can of Vienna sausages. Of course I loved Nero Wolfe and Archie Goodwin, but I'd recently discovered Dol Bonner, the female private eye he'd introduced in *The Hand in the Glove*.

Miss Osborne untied the earflaps of her hat but left them hanging down over her ears. 'Mr Stout, I'd like you to meet Mrs Louise Pearlie, my assistant. She's a dedicated reader of detective novels.'

As Stout reached out to shake my hand I quickly wiped mine on my trousers so he wouldn't feel how clammy it was.

'Nice to meet you,' he said.

'Lovely to meet you, too,' I said, managing to get the words out without stammering. 'I am a fan of your books. I admire Dol Bonner. We need more female characters in detective fiction. I hope she'll appear in more of your books.'

Stout smiled. 'I'm glad,' he said, 'I'm fond of her too. And yes, I do have future plans for her.'

I would have liked to ask him how he managed to write an entire book in thirty-five days, when he began typing knowing just a few characters and the murder victim, but I knew he was in the office on business. Stout was president of the Writers' War Board, an agency of professional writers who offered to write war propaganda for the government. He had put his own work on hold to keep himself available to the government for whatever they might need from him.

'I know you're due in General Donovan's office in a few minutes,' Miss Osborne said to Stout as we took our seats around the conference table. 'But we do have a request for you today.'

Stout pulled a reporter's notebook and a gold fountain pen out of his jacket pocket.

'We simply must have more women,' Miss Osborne said. 'The government is short of the clerical staff it needs and the Women's Army Corps hasn't met its recruitment objectives. We need a new approach to convincing women to go out to work.'

Stout glanced up. 'What do you think is the main reason women aren't responding? We need to know so we can tailor a plan.'

Miss Osborne sighed. 'We really don't know. Our recruitment ads and pamphlets cover every question we think a woman might have about working in government. Young single women respond much better than women with children, as you might guess, but we don't know how to convince them.'

'It must be the children, then,' I said. 'It's natural for mothers to want to care for their children.'

'The day nursery system is excellent,' Miss Osborne said. 'Beneficial for the children as well as the mothers.'

'Is that actually the case?' Merle asked.

'All the surveys indicate so,' Miss Osborne said. 'Children have fun and learn during the day while their mothers work, and mothers are pleased with the results.'

'What you need are stories,' Stout said. 'You can assure women their children will do well in day nurseries, but telling them won't convince them. You must show them. I'd suggest we work on some newspaper feature articles with actual women who are well pleased with the nurseries that keep their children, and perhaps some fiction short stories for the women's magazines.'

'We're willing to try any approach,' Miss Osborne said. 'Otherwise the country might need to draft women for war work.'

Stout whistled. 'That would cause an uproar.'

'Indeed it would,' Miss Osborne said.

'The Board meets in New York City next week. Faith Baldwin and Mary Roberts Rinehart are on our advisory committee. I'll ask them to recommend a campaign to the Board. We could have stories in print within six weeks or so.'

'Thank you. We'll hope for a good result,' Miss Osborne said.

'I must go to my meeting or I'll be late,' Stout said. He tore a page out of his notebook and scribbled on it before tucking the notebook back into his jacket pocket. Then he handed the page to me. It read, 'Mrs Pearlie, keep reading Dol, all best, Rex Stout.'

I'd encountered celebrities at OSS and around Washington before. I'd seen John Wayne at lunch with John Ford, who headed the OSS Film Unit, a couple of times. You couldn't miss Wayne; he towered over everyone else in the OSS cafeteria. I even had a short conversation once with Clark Gable at a party. He was sad and preoccupied, though, since his wife, Carole Lombard, had died shortly before.

But Rex Stout! Wow! And I couldn't tell a soul that I'd met him or that I'd gotten his autograph.

Officer Dickenson left the engine idling to keep the police car warm while he and Sergeant Royal waited until it was time to go to Leo Maxwell's house for their appointment. They were a bit early, and it wouldn't do to irritate rich people. They got so riled up when their schedules were disturbed. Both men lit cigarettes while they waited, filling the car with clouds of smoke.

'You've shaved,' Dickenson said to Royal, in between inhalations. 'And your tie is clean.'

'I felt it would be in my best interests to look presentable today,' Royal said. 'I expect that Leo Maxwell will have heard from his lawyer by now and will understand that he has to allow me to interview him. These are people who wear clean shirts every day, after all. They must have some familiarity with the law.'

'Good idea,' Dickenson said, glancing at his watch.

'It's still too early,' Royal said. 'Relax.'

Dickenson cranked his window down and threw out his cigarette butt. He'd parked out in front of the ugly Victorian mansion that had once been the German embassy, which was just a few houses down from the Maxwell pile. The entire German legation had been escorted out of the building a few days after Germany declared war on the United States on December 11, 1941. It had been shuttered ever since, protected by that useful neutral country, Switzerland.

'That place gives me the creeps,' he said to Royal.

'What, the old embassy?' Royal was lighting up another cigarette. 'It's just an empty building.'

'It looks like a mausoleum,' Dickenson said. 'With the windows blocked off by blackout curtains night and day. Not a human being in sight.'

'Not what it used to be,' Royal said, glancing over at the building and shrugging. 'How the mighty have fallen.'

'Do you believe the things they say about what happened there?'

'What things?'

'You know, the parties.'

'Sure,' Royal said. 'I had a buddy that did some security there on his off hours. I think the word he used was "depraved". Caviar heaped in gold dishes, champagne fountains and dancing in three different ballrooms. He said the crystal chandeliers were as big as refrigerators. The women were draped in jewels. They looked like Christmas trees with breasts, he said. And every one of the thirty bedrooms in the place was put to good use. Most of the people who went to those parties weren't even German. They were rich Americans and embassy people from friendly countries.'

'And the spying? I heard the entire top floor was full of communications equipment.'

'I wouldn't be surprised.'

'Do you believe the stories about the money?'

Royal cranked down his window and quickly threw out his cigarette butt before rolling it up again. 'That there's millions of American dollars in cash hidden inside the building somewhere? Money the Nazis used to pay all their spies and informants? Maybe.'

'You don't think the Swiss took it when they got control of the building?'

'Nah. The last thing the Swiss need is more money. They're rolling in it. They'll come out of this war richer than ever. And they'll want to hedge their bets. When the end of the war comes they'll turn over that embassy just like they got it. It's the way they are.' Royal glanced at his watch. 'Come on. Time to call on the Maxwell family.'

Merle leaned back in his chair after Rex Stout had left the conference room. A rangy Texan who'd been a newspaper illustrator before the war, he was now a forger for OSS. Honestly, the man could copy anything. He spoke and read German too, since his grandparents were immigrants and never learned English, although his Texas accent caused some hilarity among the native German speakers at OSS.

'Get yourself some more coffee,' he said. 'There's even sugar.'

I peeled off the outer layer of my clothing and poured myself a cup. It was lovely and warm in the room, thanks to the army tent stove that had been set up in a corner. The potbellied stove looked like a miniature of the big one that heated my grandparents' house for years. I'd bet anything that it was surplus from the First World War. The stovepipe ran up and out a hole that had been cut in the wall and chinked with cement. A couple of scuttles of coal sat on the floor.

'Now,' Miss Osborne said.

'What's this all about?' Merle said. 'I know there's always plenty of work to do, but shouldn't we be at home avoiding the flu and the cold for a couple of days?'

'We have an urgent project to plan,' Miss Osborne said. 'It can't wait until everyone is healthy and the weather is better.'

She pulled a file out of her bag and I reached for a notepad and pencil.

She flipped through the pages of her files and then looked up at the two of us.

'You are aware that President Roosevelt, Churchill and Stalin met in Tehran to discuss the invasion of Europe, the Second Front that must happen as soon as possible.'

'Before the Russians are defeated,' Merle said.

Miss Osborne smiled. 'The Russians will never be defeated,' she said. 'Exhausted, out of supplies, ordnance and fresh troops, yes, but never defeated.' The resilience of the Russian people and the stoicism of their troops had become legendary. Winter was their favorite season to fight, and they had begun their winter drive. The Russian people slept with their guns and ate their pets without complaint. There were rumors of Russian soldiers with eight wound stripes. And I'd heard from OSS observers who'd returned from the Russian front that as soon as a wounded Russian soldier came out of anesthesia, the orderlies threw a machine gun into bed with him, and he'd spend his convalescence taking it apart, cleaning it and reassembling it.

'Maybe only ten people in the world know the actual plan for the invasion, but we do know it will come in the spring, while the Russians can still force Hitler to stay engaged in the east,' Miss Osborne said. 'The President briefed General Eisenhower in Carthage on his way home.'

The spring! What, five months from now? How could the Allies possibly stage the invasion of a continent bristling with firepower in that amount of time!

'General Eisenhower and the military's job will be the invasion. Our job in the psychological warfare services will be to wage a war within a war, distracting Hitler and the Germans from the invasion plan. Starting now.'

'But we don't know what the plan is yet, do we?' I asked. Intense arguments took place all over Washington about the pros and cons of an invasion of France versus throwing Allied strength behind our position in Italy.

'No, but General Donovan wants us to craft a new operation, one that's simple, concrete, on the ground, that will begin to affect Axis morale. Before the holidays.'

'Ruin Christmas for the Nazis,' Merle said.

'This is what can't wait, what I want you two to start on today. We need to devise a plan and get it to London so it can be implemented immediately.'

'We know nothing about the Allied invasion plans, but we want to distract the German military and worry the German people,' I said. 'Make them feel in danger.'

'Exactly,' Miss Osborne said.

'Sure,' Merle said. 'We should be able to do that in a day.'

Miss Osborne dumped a stack of files and papers on the table. 'Here,' she said. 'This is what's going on in Europe. Let's refresh our memories first.'

The Allies hadn't invaded Fortress Europe yet, but we were already circling its walls. The Reds were somehow still holding off the Germans outside Kiev. The Fifth Army was within striking distance of Rome, planning to be there by Christmas, but their gains were measured in single miles. In August the Nazi government had moved major ministries out of Berlin to Vienna to escape RAF bombing runs over the capital city. The German military had moved resources to southern Germany and northern Italy to stop Allied forces moving north from southern Italy. There were probably fewer divisions in France now than at any time since the Germans occupied it. Which sounded to me like a good reason to invade through France.

OSS was in Europe now too. 'Blueblood Bruce', David K.E. Bruce, who had the challenging job of working with our British cousins, MI5, MI6 and the Special Operations Executive, all of which ran competing spy networks in France, headed our London office. OSS funneled piles of money to the European resistance, especially the French Maquis, to finance underground mayhem on the continent, annoying both the British and the French.

Since October, the first clandestine anti-Nazi radio station, Soldatensender Calais, broadcast a mixture of truth and fiction from England deep into Germany, reaching soldiers and citizenry alike. OSS provided a dozen writers and musicians to the radio station. Marlene Dietrich recorded special anti-Nazi songs for it in a recording studio in New York City.

OSS had a presence in the neutral countries, too. Allen

Dulles was our spymaster in Bern. Colonel Robert Solborg
commanded OSS in Lisbon, the spy capital of the world, the
European city that harbored every European who could buy,
barter, bribe or murder their way out of the occupied continent.
Lisbon groaned under the weight of frightened refugees trapped
between the Axis powers and the Atlantic Ocean. Much of
Joe's work was directed to finding the ships that would rescue
Jewish refugees and carry them to safety.

But none of this helped us with our current project, devising
a simple ground operation that would demoralize the German
people and soldiers and could be implemented before
the holidays.

By lunchtime we'd gone through every file folder on the
table and were still stumped for a new idea. MO was already
disseminating fake letters, pamphlets, rumors and newspapers, as fast as we could recruit operatives to distribute
them. Our radio stations blanketed much of Europe already.
Until we were deeper into Europe I didn't know what else
we could do.

'All right,' Miss Osborne said, removing her glasses. 'Let's
break for lunch. Any ideas?'

She was met by our silence. 'Me neither,' she said.

'I'm starving,' Merle said. 'But the last thing I want to do
is go over to the cafeteria, where flu germs are rampaging.'

'I'll go out and get sandwiches,' I said. 'I'd like the walk.'

'If you're willing to brave this cold it's fine with me,' said
Miss Osborne. 'Do you think you can find a café open?'

'The one across the street from the south gate is open. I
had breakfast there this morning,' Merle said.

'That's close by,' I said. 'What does everyone want?'

Since we never knew exactly which items on a menu would
actually be available, we ordered by exclusion.

'As long as it's not peanut butter and jelly I'm fine,'
Miss Osborne said.

'You know how I feel about cheese and pickle sandwiches.
I guess I'd prefer ham,' Merle said. 'And get some potato
chips.'

'Maybe an apple,' Miss Osborne added.

The temperature dropped precipitously as I moved out of

the warm conference room into the hallway, and I walked quickly toward my office. Pulling on my coat and the rest of my heavy clothing, I ventured outside, nodded at the guard at the gate and hurried across the street.

I stood at the counter and perused the menu. 'Three grilled ham and cheese sandwiches, please,' I said to the woman behind the counter. 'No pickles. And three bags of potato chips. To go.'

'Coming right up,' she said, passing the order through the kitchen window behind her. I unwrapped my scarf so I could breathe while I waited.

The bulky bundle alongside turned to me. 'Mrs Pearlie,' he said, in a voice muffled by his turned-up greatcoat collar, 'I thought I recognized your voice.'

'Oh,' I said, 'Mr Becker.'

'Please call me Al,' he said.

'I'm Louise.'

I wasn't exactly pleased to see one of my fellow witnesses to the discovery at the Baron Steuben Inn, but as he was waiting for his lunch too, I had no choice but to stand with him at the counter for a few minutes.

'I hope you are doing well,' he said. 'After Saturday night.'

'As well as I can be,' I said. 'You?'

Al shrugged. 'It's difficult to stop thinking about.'

'We should probably not discuss it in public.'

'I agree.'

'You're a long way from the zoo,' I said, awkwardly changing the conversation.

'I'm on my way back from delivering a stack of mail and memos to the Director's office at the Smithsonian Castle. If we sent them by interdepartmental mail they'd take a week to arrive. I have a car, so it is easy for me to drop them off during my lunch hour. I like to stop here to pick up lunch. The egg salad is delicious.'

The woman behind the counter slapped the bell and held out our paper lunch bags to us. We paid for them and rewrapped ourselves in our scarves.

Al held the door open for me as we left.

'Louise,' he said, just as I was about to cross the street.

'Yes?'

'I remember you said how much you enjoy the gorillas at the zoo.'

'I do, very much.'

'Well, we have a new baby. His name is Daudi. The public cannot view him yet, but if you come by sometime I can show him to you.'

'Really?' I said. I was sorely tempted. On the one hand I felt I shouldn't pursue a friendship with this man, especially as Sergeant Royal suspected his story, but on the other hand, well, a baby gorilla! How could it hurt?

'Just come by the administration building at the zoo any time,' he said. 'That's where my office is.'

'I will if I can,' I said. A gust of wind blew down the street; we hunkered down into our coats as we parted, Al walking toward his car while I crossed the street.

By the time I got back to the conference room the sandwiches were cold and I had an idea.

If the old German embassy was dead then the Maxwell mansion was very much alive. The upper floor was dark; Royal assumed it had been shut off to save fuel oil. But the draperies in the floor-to-ceiling ground-floor windows were wide open and the interiors blazed with light, giving Royal and Dickenson a glimpse of gleaming mahogany furniture and oil paintings stacked one on top of the other from the chair rail to the ceiling.

An elderly butler opened the door and looked down his nose at the two of them.

'Detective Sergeant Royal and Officer Dickenson to see Mr Leo Maxwell,' Royal said. 'He should be expecting us.'

'Come in,' the butler said. 'I shall tell Mr Maxwell that you are here.'

The butler left them standing in the hall to contemplate several marble statues that stood around the round foyer. A half-dozen candelabra taller than Royal stood ready to light the hall for parties. A staircase carpeted in red curled away and above them.

'Dickenson, close your mouth,' Royal said. 'You're gaping.'

Dickenson pressed his lips together. 'Sir, isn't the butler supposed to show us to a parlor or something?'

'Not us. The police are considered tradesmen.'

The butler reappeared.

'This way, please.'

He led them into a sitting room still reeling from an Art Moderne decorating spree. A breakfront with brass pulls had more curves than Ava Gardner. The curved sofa and matching club chairs, with wood trim painted black and dove-grey upholstery, reminded Royal of an elegant man's suit. No busy flowered wallpaper here. A coffee table trimmed in brass reflected light in patches on to peach-colored walls.

Maxwell leaned against the fireplace mantel. He was wearing tweed trousers, a white dress shirt with the cuffs unbuttoned and a black-and-grey Argyle sweater. To Dickenson's surprise, Gloria Scott reclined on the davenport. Her elegant lounging pajamas were cut much like Mavis Forrester's, but Scott's were silk decorated with black Chinese pagodas and red macaws, nicely accessorizing the room itself.

Royal reached for Mrs Scott's hand, which she extended to him with a nod. 'Mrs Scott,' he said, 'I must say that I am glad to see you here. Saves the police from running around all over the city looking for you.'

'It's important that no one knows she is here,' Maxwell said. 'If at all possible.'

'You see,' Scott said. 'I am divorcing my husband. My attorney tells me I should behave like a saint until the decree is final. It's bad enough that I was present at the scene of a murder that was plastered over the crime pages of all the newspapers in the city. I would hate for news that I am here with the Maxwell family to reach the papers.'

'My parents have offered Mrs Scott shelter in our home,' Maxwell said. 'Until the fuss dies down, you see. She and I are engaged. I do hope you can keep her whereabouts a secret.'

Could a couple be engaged, Dickenson wondered, if one of them was still married?

'This fuss, as you call it, is a murder investigation,' Royal said. 'Neither one of you should have avoided the police. We need your statements. I see no reason to reveal your whereabouts to the press, but I expect your full cooperation. I have questions that you simply must answer.'

'Fire away,' Maxwell said. He didn't offer them a seat, but Royal and Dickenson each took one anyway. Royal pulled out his ever-present notebook.

'When did you arrive at the bar? And by the way, why that bar?'

Maxwell shrugged. 'It's close by, just across the street. No one we know goes there. There are often photographers outside this house. You have no idea what it can be like.'

'We arrived separately,' Gloria Scott said, curling her legs up under her on the davenport. 'I took a taxi from my hotel and went in the back door. Leo met me there.'

Royal paused in his note taking. This made no sense to him. Surely these two could get a private drink somewhere other than a beat-up neighborhood bar. At a private club, or in a nook at Scott's hotel. He didn't say anything to them but filed the thought away for future reference.

'What time did you arrive?'

'Perhaps eight thirty,' Maxwell said.

'Who was there before you?'

'Everyone except the other couple. The woman with the glasses and the dark bearded man. They came in after we arrived.' Louise Pearlie and Joe Prager, Dickenson thought.

'Did you see anything suspicious at all before the body was discovered?'

Maxwell shrugged. 'No, not at all.' He looked pointedly at Scott. 'What about you, darling?'

'No, nothing.'

'Mrs Scott,' Royal continued, 'you said you came in the back door, correct?'

'Yes. So I wouldn't be seen with Leo.'

'You would have passed by the storeroom door. Did you notice if it was open or shut? Did you pass anyone in the alley on your way to the back door? Or see anyone leave the bar out the back?'

Scott frowned, then smoothed the skin between her eyes with a thumb, as if she could prevent frown lines from forming. 'I believe the storeroom door was closed,' she said. 'And I didn't see a soul in the alley.'

'Did either of you know the murder victim? Or anyone else at the bar that night?'

'No,' Maxwell and Scott said, almost simultaneously.

Royal shut his notebook and stood up. Dickenson followed suit.

'All right,' Royal said. 'I'll get these typed up and a police officer will bring copies by for you to sign. Please tell your servants to admit them. The police aren't delivery boys.'

Maxwell nodded and Royal moved forward to shake his hand. Instead he picked up a large photograph that sat on the mantelpiece near Maxwell. It showed a handsome middle-aged man dressed in white tie and tails standing next to the former German ambassador, Hans-Heinrich Dieckhoff, in an opulent drawing room. A large Maltese-style cross with a red ribbon hung from his neck.

'The resemblance is striking,' Royal said. 'Your father?'

'Yes,' Maxwell said. 'He received the Order of the German Eagle in 1937. You do understand, other prominent Americans received these medals too. Henry Ford and Charles Lindbergh were two of them. Father regrets it today, of course.'

'Of course,' Royal said. He doubted it. Otherwise he wouldn't still have the picture displayed.

Once outside in the car Royal scribbled again in his notebook. 'We need to know about the Order of the German Eagle, why it was given to Maxwell Senior. And where exactly the Maxwells get their money,' he said.

'Do you think maybe they're Nazi sympathizers?'

'They were before the war, that's obvious from the picture. But so were plenty of other big shots. Let's not make any snap judgments. Find out the facts first.'

SIX

'Why reinvent the wheel?' I said, finishing the cup of hot coffee I'd poured to drink with my lunch. 'What do you mean?' Miss Osborne said, neatly wiping her mouth. Merle tossed his wadded-up sandwich wrapper into a ball and threw it into a trash can across the room.

'Let's adapt something that already works,' I said.

Merle crossed his legs, showing his tooled leather cowboy boots. 'Like what?'

'Like this,' I said, flipping through the stack of folders we'd been through for the file I needed. 'Here,' I said. '"The Devil's Brigade". They leave these calling cards with the German soldiers they've killed.' The Devil's Brigade was the nickname of the First Special Service Force, an elite American–Canadian commando unit trained to fight in winter conditions. At this moment the brigade was deployed at the German winter front line in the mountains of Italy. Breaking through that line would allow the Allied forces to advance to Rome.

A commander of the Devil's Brigade had devised his own bit of propaganda warfare. On the corpse of every German soldier his troops left a calling card, a cardboard square printed with a red arrow, the emblem of the brigade, and the phrase *Das dicke Ende kommt noch!* – 'The worst is yet to come!'.

Miss Osborne read the contents of the folder, passing each page to Merle. When she finished she looked up but past me, thinking. Merle finished reading and shoved the last page back into the file folder. 'But this isn't a Devil's Brigade operation,' he said.

'That's not a problem,' Miss Osborne said. 'We'll just steal the idea.'

'But the Germans know perfectly well the Devil's Brigade is in the mountains of Italy, not in France or Denmark or anywhere else.'

'We'll adapt it,' I said. 'We'll use the phrase and change the symbol to something universal. Then we'll distribute the cards to the resistance in Europe. French, Danish, Greek, wherever our operatives can get the cards. That way they'll be distributed all over the continent.'

'Louise, this is good,' Miss Osborne said. 'Very good. We'll scatter these all over Europe and the Germans won't know who is responsible for them. Do you have an idea for a symbol?'

'I'm afraid not,' I said.

'A bomb falling?' Merle asked.

'Too specific,' Miss Osborne said.

'An explosion?' I said.

'It needs to be really scary,' Merle said. 'Evocative. Like the boogeyman.' He spread apart his hands in frustration. 'I don't know enough German psychology to suggest anything.'

'Something that a German would recognize as terrifying,' Miss Osborne said. 'We're going to need to take advantage of your research skills here, Louise. I'll take this idea to General Donovan so he can present it to the Planning Committee. Merle, you get to work on the layout, and Louise, find us a symbol!'

The reading room of the Registry, the library of OSS, my old stomping ground, was as empty as the rest of the capital city. For once it was easy to find a seat at one of the long tables without waiting. It was lovely to be a visitor, requesting files and books, instead of one of the girls who fetched, returned and filed all day.

Right away I found a good candidate for a symbol for the cards Miss Osborne would suggest to the Planning Committee as morale-busters on the ground in Europe.

Krampus, a horned, devil-like creature with a long pre-Christian folklore history, punished naughty children at Christmas. Hairy, black, with one cloven hoof and one human foot, he had the horns of a goat and a long red pointed tongue that hung from his mouth. He carried a bundle of birch rods or a whip to beat children with, and sometimes a washtub for carrying them off to Hell. He was a direct descendant of the pagan Horned God of Witches, then assimilated into Christian folklore as a variation of the Devil. He was an ugly, evil-looking creature, and one the German people would remember from terrifying childhood folk stories. I thought he would do nicely.

I traced a drawing of Krampus from the book on German folklore I'd been reading, so that Miss Osborne and Merle could get an idea of how ghastly a creature he was. If we decided that Krampus was indeed the symbol we were looking for, Merle could come to the reading room himself and find examples to copy.

It had taken only an hour for me to find my symbol, and I felt as though I could take a short break and do some research of my own. I was curious about the Maxwell family. The proximity of the Baron Steuben Inn, the old German embassy and the Maxwell home had begun to prick my overactive imagination, and I wondered just how much time the Maxwells had spent with their Nazi neighbors before the war.

I didn't want to request the Maxwell file formally. It would be better if there was no record in the logbooks of my interest. So I went off into the maze of file cabinets myself. No one knew them better than me anyway. I had an official visitor badge and was well known to everyone who worked in the Registry. Because of the shortage of workers it wasn't strange that I would be looking through the files myself.

I pulled a thick file labeled 'Maxwell family' out of an 'M' file cabinet. It was filled with newspaper and magazine clippings. In short order I learned that Leo's parents' names were Gene and Lola and that he had twin sisters, Anne and Mary, both married off to appropriate husbands. The photographs of their double wedding in the society pages of the *Herald* were just stunning. The girls, as they were called in the article, wore matching designer gowns of satin and lace with flapper-style rhinestone headbands. Leo was a handsome best man in his tuxedo, standing between the grooms. He was described as a 'championship tennis and polo player'. Apparently he neither attended college nor worked. The wedding had taken place at the Lutheran church around the corner from the Maxwell mansion. The reception was held in the ballroom of the Mayflower Hotel.

Another clipping showed the German ambassador pinning a medal on Gene Maxwell. A small group of men looked on. Including, I noticed, Henry Ford and Charles Lindbergh, both prominent Nazi sympathizers before the war. Lindbergh had met with Hitler and almost moved to Germany in 1938, but public criticism of him by President Roosevelt compelled him to resign his Army Air Forces commission and remain in the United States. In the 1920s Henry Ford published an anti-Semitic newspaper, the *Dearborn Independent*, and was mentioned with admiration by Adolf Hitler in *Mein Kampf*. Now both men, of course, had changed their minds about Hitler. Lindbergh was distinguishing himself in the Pacific war and Ford claimed he knew nothing of the content of his newspaper.

As for the Maxwells' fortune, they made it in the Midwest growing feed for cattle and hogs. In the late thirties they sold their acreage and feedlots and moved to DC, where they were welcomed into society and went to parties at, among other places, the German embassy.

All of which was very intriguing, but not unique. Much of the wealthy class of the United States had been taken with fascism and Hitler. As had the upper classes in Britain. The Duke of Windsor was so well known for his interest in Nazism that the Prime Minister, Churchill, appointed him Governor of the Bahamas to get him out of Europe. He was concerned that the Duke would be kidnapped by the Nazis and used for propaganda purposes.

It took me just a few more minutes to find out about the Order of the German Eagle. It was the highest Nazi decoration given to prominent foreigners who were sympathetic to Nazism. Other Americans who received it were Thomas J. Watson, chairman of IBM, and James Mooney, General Motors' director of overseas operations. I understood that the Nazi Party tried to influence important Americans to pressure Roosevelt to stay out of the war. What was so ironic was how much their companies benefited financially from the US entering the war.

I closed the file and carefully replaced it. I knew from experience the chaos that could emerge from misfiled information. If you couldn't find it, it just didn't exist. Which made me think of Sergeant Royal. I was sure he would be interested in what I'd found out about the Maxwell family, and I wondered if it would be OK for me to call him. I'd done this research to satisfy my own curiosity, it wasn't part of my job, but still I'd used files from the OSS Registry. This was something I'd have to think about.

Back at OSS I presented 'Krampus' to Miss Osborne and Merle. They agreed that he was the perfect symbol for our calling card. What could better illustrate a slogan like 'the worst is yet to come' than a hairy black devil with a whip resurrected from the darkest childhood fears of the average German? Within weeks resistance fighters of all nationalities would have a supply of these cards so they could tuck them into the pockets of the corpses of the German soldiers they killed. Krampus' relationship to Christmas made the symbolism even better, since he was the creature who brought naughty children their lumps of coal.

'This should work very well,' Miss Osborne said. 'I think General Donovan will agree. Merle, how soon can you do a mockup of the card?'

'By noon tomorrow,' he said, 'no problem. I'll get started right now.'

After Merle left Miss Osborne went to the stove, opened the door and shoveled in more coal. While I was gone someone had brought cots to the room and leaned them up against the wall. A box of blankets and pillows sat beside them. We really were going to sleep in the office tonight.

Miss Osborne noticed my bemused expression and grinned at me. 'Sort of like summer camp,' she said.

'If only we had marshmallows,' I said. 'We could toast them over the fire.'

To my surprise Miss Osborne opened a door, pulled out a *Do Not Disturb* sign and hung it on the doorknob outside the conference room. 'We need to talk, Louise,' she said.

I felt my heart rate quicken. 'Is something wrong?'

'Nothing you've done,' she said. 'Sit down.' I did, and she sat in the chair beside me. She looked slightly silly, such a serious expression while still wearing that ridiculous hat.

'It's about the murder victim at the Baron Steuben Inn. I've talked to General Donovan, and he's authorized me to tell you that the dead man was one of ours.'

'Oh no!'

'Yes, I'm afraid so. Floyd Stinson was the custodian of the German embassy, one of several American employees. He'd worked there since 1931. The Swiss kept him on because he knew the building so well. We recruited him as soon as the Germans left and the Swiss took possession in December of 1941.'

'To do what?'

Miss Osborne smiled despite the seriousness of our conversation. 'To spy on a building,' she said. 'We instructed him, basically, to poke around whenever he could get away with it – without the Swiss knowing, of course. To look for documents that might have been left behind. To investigate the third floor – which was locked – if he could, where the communication center was.'

'What about the money?' I asked.

'What money?'

'I heard the Germans kept several million American dollars in cash in the embassy. To bribe people with. To pay spies.'

'Nonsense,' Miss Osborne said. 'That's just a silly rumor. Stinson was searching for intelligence, nothing more. Floyd had to be careful, of course,' she continued.

A Swiss caretaker lived at the embassy. The United States Army kept two guards with dogs on duty outside the building twenty-four hours a day. When they took possession, the Swiss had inventoried the contents of the massive mansion, both embassy property and the personal possessions of individuals that were left behind. Floyd did deliver to OSS some informative documents, codebooks, personal letters, logs of visitors to the embassy and similar items. They were photographed so he could return them. 'He was very useful to us,' Miss Osborne said. 'And now he's been murdered.'

'You think his death is related to his work for OSS?'

'We don't know. And General Donovan, of course, wants to find out. Even more important, we don't want the FBI to learn we were running an agent inside the country.'

Counterintelligence was the prerogative of the FBI, not OSS. If Director Hoover knew OSS had an agent inside the German embassy he would use that information against Donovan. The two men waged an incessant war against each other for President Roosevelt's ear, and this could give Hoover an edge.

'So Sergeant Royal can't find out that Floyd Stinson worked for OSS.'

'No,' she said, 'or he'll be obliged to notify the FBI. We need you to use your friendship with Royal to keep tabs on this murder investigation. Royal will find out soon that Stinson worked at the German embassy.' When the FBI ran his finger-prints, I thought.

Finally it made some sense that no one in the bar had known what Stinson did for a living. He would have kept it as quiet as possible. It was a legitimate job, but one that would inevit-ably provoke questions. I could imagine what Walt and Chippy would have had to say if they'd known that Stinson kept the pipes from freezing at the old German embassy.

I realized that I could use the information I'd found about the Maxwell family to make contact with Royal. I knew this was my job, but I felt badly about using him.

'I can call Royal tomorrow, invite him for lunch or something,' I said.

'Good,' Miss Osborne said. She went to the door and removed the *Do Not Disturb* sign. 'Want to eat in the cafeteria tonight? They're offering two of my favorites, tuna croquettes and Hawaiian chicken.'

We were a woebegone group at dinner. There were never many people in the OSS cafeteria at dinnertime, but tonight we only filled two tables. The powers that be had decided not to waste heating fuel on such a small crowd, so the food cooled off on the trip from the cafeteria line to our seats.

I scraped the canned pineapple off my 'Hawaiian' chicken before eating it. I should have had the tuna croquettes. The ubiquitous mashed potatoes and carrots accompanied both entrées. It would keep us alive until morning, but that was about all.

When we returned to the conference room Miss Osborne, Merle and I spent the rest of the evening making a dent in the work that had piled up in the branch during the flu outbreak. I spent the evening in the mailroom, sorting the contents of a couple of pouches of mail, both diplomatic and otherwise, and stuffing it into the correct individual mail slots. Miss Osborne waded through a stack of memos sent to our branch by Donovan's office. Merle spent the evening drawing Krampus in several disturbing poses so that we could pick out the one we wanted to illustrate our 'calling card'.

'You realize,' Miss Osborne said as she dropped into the mailroom to check on me, 'that we're missing Burns and Allen tonight.' Along with the rest of the country, I was a devoted listener to the CBS radio show featuring husband-and-wife team George Burns and Gracie Allen. Burns was the straight man and Gracie played his silly, addle-brained wife.

'If that's not a sacrifice for our country I don't know what is,' I said.

About eleven Miss Osborne and I brushed our teeth in the girls' bathroom and tucked ourselves into our cots, fully dressed. A reticent WAC from the Codes and Communications branch who took a handie-talkie to bed with her in case she was needed during the night joined us. It was the size of a loaf of bread with an antenna that jutted a couple of feet past the head of her cot. Merle slept in the artists' workroom with a half-dozen other men.

'So,' Sergeant Royal said, 'to what do I owe the honor of this luncheon invitation? Could it be that you want to pump me about the Stinson murder?'

'Certainly not,' I said. 'I'm just doing my civic duty. I found some things out about the Maxwells I thought you might want to know. Nothing related to my job,' I added. 'But let's order first.'

We studied the café menu until our waitress arrived.

'Are you buying?' Royal asked me. 'I understand that you government girls make good money.'

'Of course. I invited you. You can have anything you want. I'm rolling in dough.'

'Then I'll have vegetable soup and a grilled cheese sandwich,' he said.

'I'll have the same,' I said, closing my menu and handing it to the waitress.

Royal began to pull his cigarettes out of his pocket and then paused. 'You'd prefer me not to smoke, wouldn't you?'

'If you can bear it,' I said. 'It makes my throat sore.'

'You must be the only person in this town who doesn't smoke.'

'Sometimes I think so,' I said. 'And sometimes I really wish I could. People seem to find it so relaxing.'

Royal grinned at me. 'There's always drinking.'

'There is that. I love martinis.' If only my parents could see me now. They would be stunned. There were worse crutches, like Phoebe's Nembutal. I borrowed one from her occasionally. And the laudanum she took for her splitting headaches. Although now that Milt was home and she had just one son in combat Phoebe seemed less unnerved. And what was Ada's excessive partying, if it wasn't a distraction from her constant worry that someone would find out she was still married to Rein Hermann, a pilot in the Luftwaffe?

The waitress brought us our drinks, a Coke for me and coffee for Royal.

'So what's up?' Royal asked.

'I was doing some work at the Registry,' I said, lowering my voice. 'I had a few minutes to spare and decided to satisfy my curiosity about the Maxwell family. So I checked them out.'

'It's good to have friends in high places. I hope you didn't do anything you shouldn't.'

'No, I used nothing confidential, just a clipping file. The Maxwell family were Nazi sympathizers before the war. Gene Maxwell, Leo's father, was awarded the Order of the German Eagle by the Germans in 1937.'

'That I knew. I saw a photograph of the ceremony when I was getting Leo's statement. But I don't know what the medal was for.'

'It was the highest decoration a foreign civilian could receive from Germany,' I said. 'Given to prominent Nazi sympathizers all over the world. The Maxwell family made a huge fortune in the Midwest, growing feed for cattle and running feedlots.

They sold their business and moved to Washington, DC. Looks like they wanted to be at the center of political power.'

'There's no telling what Nazi nastiness that man financed,' Royal said. We paused our conversation while the waitress placed our orders on the table in front of us.

I tucked into my soup and sandwich. I was hungry after the poor meals I'd been getting in the OSS cafeteria. Breakfast this morning was stale cereal, and I intended to forget last night's dinner. In between mouthfuls I finished briefing Royal on what I'd found out about the Maxwells.

'That medal Gene Maxwell got – Henry Ford and Charles Lindbergh got it too,' I said.

'I know. Leo said his father regretted it. I bet he does. I doubt he thinks he was wrong, though. Just happened to wind up on the wrong side of history.'

'The clipping file was full of society page stories,' I said. 'You should have seen the photos of the Maxwell daughters' wedding. The old man must have spent a bundle on it. Oh, and it took place at the Lutheran church around the corner from the old German embassy. The reception was at the Mayflower Hotel.'

'I wonder if the Maxwell family still has German connections. It's odd how this murder seems to revolve around the German embassy.'

'I thought the same thing,' I said. 'The Baron Steuben Inn is right across the street. Al Becker told me that it used to stock all the best German beers, so I expect a lot of people from the embassy drank there. The Lutheran church on the corner received donations from Germany, granted before the First World War. The Maxwell daughters married there. And the Maxwells themselves live in a mansion down the street.'

The waitress arrived to pick up our plates.

'I'm still starving,' I said to Royal. 'Do you have time for dessert?'

'You still buying?'

'Sure.'

The waitress recited the dessert choices. 'Chocolate war cake, carrot spice cake and pumpkin pie.'

'I'm not sick of pumpkin yet, so I guess I'll have pie,' Royal said.

'I'll take a slice of war cake,' I said.

After the waitress left Royal cast his eyes around the room to see if there was anyone nearby before speaking. 'Since you've shared information with me, I'll share mine with you,' he said. 'I'd like your take on it. The connection of this murder to the German embassy is stronger than you know. My friend at the FBI hurried through the background checks I requested. Our murder victim, Floyd Stinson, was the longtime custodian of the embassy. He was a fine American fellow, he just happened to get a job there in 1931. Jobs were mighty scarce then. When the Swiss took charge of the embassy in 1941 he stayed on at their request.' This I knew already from Miss Osborne but I feigned surprise, and kept my mouth shut about the rest of what she'd told me. What would Royal think if he knew Stinson worked for us, and how would that affect his thinking about the murder? It certainly affected mine. I found myself feeling guilty withholding information from Sergeant Royal that might be relevant to his murder investigation, but I had no choice.

'Stinson lived at a boarding house a couple of streets south of the embassy. He'd lived there for years. We searched his room with a fine-tooth comb and found nothing but personal possessions. His landlady said he went home to his family farm in Maryland on summer weekends and holidays. There was a stack of *Farm Journal* magazines a foot high on his dresser.'

The waitress brought our desserts. The pie came without whipped cream and the cake without icing, but both tasted fine.

'And there's something else,' Royal said. 'About Al Becker.'

'Al? I liked him.'

Royal snorted. 'When he was explaining his background to us he neglected to say that the job he had when he first got to the States was as a bicycle messenger for the German embassy. He was there for years. Until he left to work for the zoo in thirty-three. Which means . . .' He looked at me expectantly.

'Oh my God!' I said. 'He had to have known Floyd Stinson. If Stinson started working there in thirty-one, and Al left in thirty-three, their service overlapped!'

'Becker told me a blatant lie. That he knew nothing about Stinson's life. He led me to believe they had become chess partners recently. You do see what that means?'

'I do,' I said. 'He wants to hide his background at the German embassy. I can understand that, we're at war, but he must have known you'd find out eventually. Do you think he's involved with Stinson's murder?'

'I don't know enough to say yet. It certainly makes me suspicious.'

After I paid our chit Royal and I left and stood for a few minutes together on the sidewalk before parting. It was still cold, but it was midday and the sun was shining brightly, giving us hope that the weather would break soon. Since our conversation at lunch I'd been wondering if I should tell Royal something else. I touched his arm.

'Sergeant,' I said, 'I ran into Al Becker at a lunch counter yesterday. He invited me to come by the zoo any time. He said he'd give me a tour.'

Royal grabbed me by both arms, dropping his cane on to the sidewalk in the process. 'Louise!' he said. 'You've got to go. He'll talk to you more freely than to the police.'

'I don't know,' I said. 'I don't know if I can get away from work. We're understaffed because of the flu.'

'Of course you can. You're good at this. Please, it could be so useful. Al won't be on guard with you. Especially if he's sweet on you.'

It hadn't occurred to me that Al's invitation might have a romantic purpose. Swell. This was just what I needed.

'I'll see what I can do,' I said.

'Call me and let me know. Let me give you my home telephone number.'

I waited while he scribbled on his notepad, then ripped the page out and handed it to me.

'I'm not promising anything,' I said.

'That's OK. Just let me know what happens.' Royal leaned over to pick up his cane but couldn't bend his knees far enough

to reach it, frustration and pain showing in his face. I picked
it up and handed it to him.

Miss Osborne was beside herself, if Miss Osborne could ever
be said to be beside herself.

'My goodness, Louise!' she said to me. Then she got up
and closed the conference room door, hanging out the *Do Not
Disturb* sign again. 'I'll be glad when the weather breaks and
we can get back into our own offices.' She took her seat again
and picked up a pencil and steno pad, peering at me over her
glasses. She'd removed her woolly *ushanka* so she looked less
like a myopic sheep.

'Let me see if I understand,' she said. 'This Al Becker
person, who now works at the National Zoo, was a bicycle
messenger at the German embassy from the time he immigrated after World War I until 1933. He must have known
our operative, Floyd Stinson, the custodian, who began work
at the embassy in 1931. The two men played chess regularly at
the Baron Steuben Inn, which was the local pub for many
of the Germans before the war because of its beer selection.
Am I correct so far?'

'Yes,' I said.

'Since the war began Stinson had worked undercover for
us, mining the embassy building for information under the
noses of its Swiss caretakers. Saturday night you and your
friend Mr Prager were in the bar when Stinson's body was
discovered by – who was it?'

'Walt, the bus driver.'

'The barkeep was too frightened to call the police until after
the bar closed. Stupid boy.'

'He'd been ill,' I said. 'He was afraid of losing his job. He
was just doing what he thought his boss wanted him to.'

'Still, it was stupid. Anyway, then, when the customers in
the bar were questioned, they insisted they didn't know much
about Stinson. And Al Becker said he had just recently met
the man and didn't know where he worked. Am I right?'

'Yes, ma'am,' I said. 'And some of the other people in
the bar had connections to the German embassy. Leo
Maxwell's father was pro-Nazi and hobnobbed with the

German ambassador. He received the Order of the German Eagle from him. Heck, even Walt was a regular. His route on Massachusetts Avenue took him past the embassy every day for years. He and Chippy routinely met at the Baron Steuben for drinks on Saturday nights.'

'I need some coffee,' Miss Osborne said.

'I'll get it,' I said. At the coffee pot I poured two cups. Our day's allotment of sugar was gone so I just added milk to both of them.

'I wish this had a slosh of bourbon in it,' Miss Osborne said as she took the cup from me.

'Sergeant Royal doesn't know that Stinson worked for us,' I added. 'He searched Stinson's room in his boarding house thoroughly and found nothing but personal stuff. And magazines on farming. His landlady said he went home to his family's farm in Maryland every chance he got.'

'Thank God,' Miss Stinson said. 'Let's pray your friend Sergeant Royal continues to accept that. If our involvement gets out you'll be able to smell the stink all the way to the White House. Let me think for a minute.' She scribbled in her steno pad for a few minutes, and then looked up at me.

'There's no question,' she said. 'You must accept Al Becker's invitation to visit the zoo. Make friends with him. As Sergeant Royal said, pump him for information.'

She was right; whether I liked it or not, I had to do this. I felt like a rat, letting Sergeant Royal think I was working for him while reporting directly back to Miss Osborne. The man trusted me with the details of this case and I was sneaking around behind his back on behalf of OSS. I wasn't lying to him exactly, but I wasn't telling him what I knew about Floyd Stinson, either.

The Connecticut Avenue bus stopped at the entrance to the National Zoo. Al was waiting for me at the bus stop and gave me his hand to step off the bottom step. He seemed very pleased to see me and I felt another pang of guilt, and a bit of trepidation. I sincerely hoped that Al had no romantic intentions. I was willing to do almost anything Miss Osborne asked me – my

job was important to me – but I disliked deceiving the man.
Even if he was a murderer.

'I'm glad the weather is better today,' Al said. 'It will make
our tour much more enjoyable.'

'Thank you for doing this,' I said. 'I know it was last minute.
My boss gave me the afternoon off because I worked so many
hours when our staff started dropping like flies with the flu.'

'No problem,' Al said. 'I've worked a lot of extra hours too.
That's what we get for being healthy, I suppose.'

He led me over to an odd-looking little vehicle. It was more
like a cart, actually, with two seats, three wheels and a steering
stick.

'This beats walking,' Al said, offering me a seat.

'What on earth is it?'

'A golf cart. It was invented out in California for golfers
who can't walk the course. We have three. They're godsends.
They get us around the grounds without using much gas. They
only go about fifteen miles an hour, so they are wonderful for
giving tours to special people.'

So I was a special person? I resolved again to keep my
distance. My plan was to be very friendly, but with no hint of
romance.

Al got into the cart beside me and turned a key in the
ignition. The cart started with a lurch and we tootled down
the tree-lined driveway toward the main zoo compound.

'Do you know anything about the history of the zoo?'
he asked.

'Not really. Just that it's part of the Smithsonian.'

'You're correct about that. The first zoo was right on the
Mall in front of the Smithsonian Castle. The animals were
kept in cages and corrals for people to see. It was very primi-
tive, as you can imagine. Then when the government bought
the land that became Rock Creek Park, they earmarked a parcel
north of the Taft Bridge for the zoo. Now, thanks to the Works
Progress Administration, which constructed four new buildings
for us, we have a modern zoo inhabited by more than twenty-
five hundred animals.'

'I love it,' I said. 'I'd never been to a zoo until I moved
here.'

'Most of the animals are inside because of the cold weather,' he said, pulling over to an outdoor area of rocks and water. 'But the seals and beavers are in their element.'

For a few minutes we watched the animals. Two beavers were building a dam, industriously delivering mud to the structure and then patting it into place with their flat tails.

'Once they're done with this dam their zookeeper will tear it down. Dams block the flow of water and mess up the pumps. But the beavers don't seem to mind. They just build them up all over again.'

Back in the golf cart we continued down the road until we came to the building that housed the great apes. We pulled over and parked. Al again gave me his hand to help me out of the cart. The man had manners, I gave him that. As we passed by the famous bronze statue of an anteater I felt my pulse begin to race. How silly, I was more excited about seeing a baby gorilla than I was worried about being part of a murder investigation!

Al opened the heavy door for me and I went inside the building. 'The mother and baby are in a private room, we'll go there, but let's take a look at the whole family first.'

I found myself in front of the barred wall that separated spectators from the great apes. The other three walls were constructed from cinder blocks, with a doorway that led to an outside play area. The cage was huge, but it still seemed too small for the animals in it. Much as I loved watching them I was bothered by their confinement. A big wooden structure in the middle gave them something to climb on. The cement floor was thickly covered in straw. A riotous jungle, populated by giraffes and zebras, was painted in bright colors on the back wall. I wondered if the apes were intelligent enough to miss their home in Africa.

I found myself gripping the handrail as Sultan, the big silverback, approached the bars of the cage and latched on to them, cocking his head to regard me. His dark brown, liquid eyes fixed on me as if he was curious about me. I had been taught not to believe in evolution, but I couldn't mistake the feeling of kinship that looking into Sultan's eyes gave me. It made me wonder.

Sultan was an enormous, powerful animal. I remembered reading about an incident when he became so enraged at a zoo visitor making faces at him that the building had to be emptied until he calmed down. He bruised himself throwing his body up against the bars trying to get at his tormenter.

Two of Sultan's 'wives', as the newspapers insisted on calling them, and a half-grown son comprised the rest of Sultan's family. Another 'wife', Eshe, and her new baby, Daudi, had been sequestered after the birth.

'Ready to see the baby?' Al asked.

'Yes, please!'

Al led me to an inconspicuous door toward the back of the building. He had to force the doorknob up and push hard to get the door open. 'This has been broken for weeks. I've put a work order in but we're short on maintenance men and I don't know when it will get fixed. It's not safe, anyone could come in here.'

Inside the small room cluttered with bags of animal feed, crates of vegetables, water buckets and other equipment was a cage about the size of a small car. A large window at the back of the cage looked out over the gorilla play area. A few tree branches and a rubber ball crowded the floor. A female gorilla clutching her tiny baby curled up in a nest of straw in a corner. The baby gorilla's miniature hands wrapped around her neck just like a human baby holding on to its mother.

'Meet Eshe and Daudi,' Al said.

'The baby is adorable,' I said. I went right up to the cage.

'Don't put your hands inside,' Al said.

Daudi stretched out a hand toward me, and it was all I could do not to try to touch him. His little eyes sparkled at me, and the furrows in his head made him look like a deep thinker. His mother kept her eye on me, but didn't seem concerned about their safety.

'Here,' Al said, handing me an apple he'd rummaged out of a box, 'just roll this into the cage and watch what happens.'

When the apple came rolling across the cage floor Eshe leaped from the nest with Daudi hanging on to her for dear life. She scooped up the apple, went back to her nest and crunched on it happily.

'Why do you have to isolate them?' I asked. 'Would the others hurt the baby?'

'Not on purpose,' Al said. 'All primates love their babies. But gorillas roughhouse, and Daudi could be injured accidentally. So we'll wait until he's about three months old before we introduce him to the troop. He'll be able to fend for himself by then.'

Al drove me back to the bus stop in the golf cart. 'Listen,' he said, as he handed me down from the cart, 'I can have the whole afternoon off. Why don't you come back with me to my place for a cup of coffee or tea? And I've got cookies you could help me eat.'

I must have looked alarmed, because he grinned at me. 'Never fear,' he said, 'my intentions are honorable. I'd appreciate your company. I don't have much of a social life. Most of my old friends in my building ignore me now because I'm German.'

'Well,' I said, 'I don't know.' But I did know. I was going. We hadn't talked yet about Stinson's murder, and that was the reason I was here.

'Besides, I'm sure you must have a boyfriend,' Al said.

'I do,' I said. 'I'm meeting him for dinner.' I had no plans to meet Joe soon, but I wanted to put a time limit on this visit. 'But there's plenty of time for cookies. I'd be happy to come.'

'Good! My car is in the parking lot near the Director's office. It's just a short walk.'

'My goodness!' I said when I saw Al's car. It was a Ford convertible roadster, cobalt blue with a white top. Late thirties, I thought.

'Like it?' he asked.

'Who wouldn't!'

'Hop in,' he said, opening the door for me. I slid on to the black leather seat. Al joined me on the driver's side. 'This is my pride and joy,' he said. 'I bought it in 1938, after my wife died, hoping to cheer myself up.'

'I'm sorry about your wife,' I said. 'I'm a widow myself. My husband died of pneumonia before the war.'

'We both know how hard it is, then,' he said.

'Yes.' It might sound insensitive of me, but the worst part

about Bill's death was losing my independence, my adulthood even. I had to move out of the apartment over the Western Union telegraph office where Bill worked and back into my childhood bedroom. Even though I had a junior college business degree I never had a job. I graduated during the Depression when there were few jobs. Anyway, Bill and I married – we'd been childhood sweethearts – and only one person in a family was permitted to work. When I returned home after his death I was expected to pitch into the family business, a smelly fish camp that I loathed, without compensation. I had no money of my own and no privacy. It seemed as though my only hope for a better life was to marry for a second time. Certainly my parents urged me to look for a husband – any single man with a job would do. Then the war came. I found a good job of my own at the Wilmington Shipbuilding Company and then moved to Washington, DC, many miles and a world away from coastal North Carolina. I loved my family, but I sure would hate to go home for anything other than a visit. Doing well in my current position was the only way I could think of to be employable after the war. Which reminded me, I was supposed to be questioning Al, not becoming his friend. Strolling about the zoo and eating cookies was just my cover.

We parked in front of a handsome apartment building just across the street from the Wardman Park Hotel. It was mere feet away from the entrance to the Taft Bridge. You could stand on the bridge and look north to the zoo grounds and south to the thick vegetation and tall trees of the park many feet below.

'What a fine building,' I said to Al, as he locked up his car.

'Thanks,' he said. 'It was built by the Woodward family, you know, of Woodward & Lothrop. They wanted a place to live away from downtown.'

Colorful tile and plaster columns in a rococo style framed the entrance door of carved wood. Inside in the lobby columns with the same rococo design reached to the tall ceiling. Al called the lift and threw open a polished brass door when it arrived with a clang. When we entered a woman in a smart coat and hat was already inside. Al tipped his hat to her. 'Hello,

Maureen,' he said. She didn't answer him, just scowled, and followed that insult by looking me over from head to foot and then turning away.

She got off on the fifth floor. 'Sorry,' Al said. 'She was one of my wife's best friends. Thank goodness Mary didn't live long enough to go through this.'

'Is there nothing you can do?' I asked.

'I'm afraid not,' he answered. 'Many of my friends just melted away when the war began. There's a men's club in the basement of the building, with a bar and card tables. I have been told I'm not welcome there. I can't seem to prove to them that I'm a real American. I'm too old to join the military. The Civil Defense Corps rejected my application.'

We got off on the seventh floor. Al led me to a door down the hall, taking out a key to unlock it. 'It's just a one-bedroom,' he said. 'That's all I need now.' We went inside his small apartment. It was modest but nicely decorated.

'Let me take your coat,' he said. 'Make yourself comfortable.' I shrugged off my coat, tucking my scarf and gloves in a pocket, and he hung it on a coatrack near the door. I sat on a comfortable chair while he went into the kitchen to fix coffee. I noticed that he was a reader. A short stack of paperback books rested on the table next to my chair. *The Ox-Bow Incident*, bookmarked with an envelope, topped the pile.

'I don't want to sound like I'm whining,' Al said from the kitchen. 'It could be much worse. I could still be in Germany, living under the Nazis. I'm treated well at the zoo, and I have a few good friends left.'

He brought out a plate of cookies. 'Oatmeal molasses cookies, no sugar needed,' he said.

'That's too many for me,' I said.

'Please eat,' he said. 'I like to bake, and I can't eat it all myself. Although sometimes I take leftovers to work.'

I took a bite. They were delicious.

'These are so good. I might be able to finish the plate after all,' I said.

'Good.' Al took a cookie too, then sipped at his coffee. But then he put down his cup and folded his arms into his body.

'Louise,' he said. 'I confess that I asked you here today for more than an afternoon visit.'

Oh no! He did have romantic intentions!

'I lied to the police, and to you, and to the other witnesses at the bar when Floyd died. When he was murdered.' He squeezed his eyes closed for a minute, as if struggling not to shed tears. 'It was a lie of omission,' he said. 'But still a lie. I was afraid that if I told the police they might suspect I was involved in Floyd's death. I wasn't, and naturally when your friend Sergeant Royal finds out, as he will soon, he will probably be even more suspicious of me.' Royal already did know what I expected Al to reveal to me, but I didn't tell Al that.

'You're not obliged to confess anything to me, I'm not the police,' I said, hoping that Al would confide even more to me than he would want the police to know.

'What I neglected to tell Royal,' he continued, 'was that when I came to the States after the First World War I worked for the German embassy. For over ten years, first as a bicycle messenger and then as the nighttime telephone operator. I knew Floyd well for the two years that our service overlapped. We played chess often even then.'

'I see,' I said.

'I was just a boy when I enlisted in Kaiser Wilhelm's army. The war was a nightmare. I found myself in the trenches, living in mud and filth like a rat in a city sewer. I wore a gas mask even when I slept. Once when the French broke through and rushed my position I shot and bayoneted . . . I don't know, several French soldiers, most of them boys like me.'

'How awful.'

'When the war was over Germany was mayhem. The economy was destroyed and people were starving. I had no family so I happily came to the States to work in our embassy. After I'd been here for a few months I had no intention of returning to Germany. And I never have and never will.'

'And you haven't told Royal this?'

'No. I plan to tomorrow. I was a fool to keep this from him. I had no reason to kill Floyd. We just played chess. We met at the Baron Steuben because all of us, the German embassy employees, once drank there for the German beer and schnapps.

The bar didn't have meals, but they brought in pretzels and bread baked at a German bakery and imported cheese and sausages, too. I kept going there after I left the embassy to see my friends, that's all. After this war started I stopped, but then the bar abandoned everything German and I began to meet Floyd there for chess again.'

'I understand, but the police are bound to suspect you.'

'You were there. Wasn't I stunned when I found Floyd's body?'

'Yes, yes you were.'

'And I came into the bar long after it opened. When was I supposed to have killed Floyd? You'd think that if I had I wouldn't have shown up at all.'

'Thank you for telling me,' I said. 'I'm sure when you tell Sergeant Royal the truth that will work in your favor.'

'I hope so.'

I knew I should stay objective, but I believed him. The fact that he didn't tell Royal that he had worked at the embassy, and with Floyd, wasn't evidence. Without a motive or opportunity it meant nothing.

I parted from Al with a handshake at the door of his building, refusing his offer of a lift home. I wanted to be alone to think. It wasn't dusk yet, and not as cold as it had been, so I decided to walk across the Taft Bridge to the bus stop on the other side to catch a bus back to the OSS compound.

The Taft Bridge was a glorious structure, an arched bridge built in Classical Revival style. It carried Connecticut Avenue over Rock Creek Gorge, towering many feet above Rock Creek and the park. Two pairs of stone lions stood guard, each pair over an entrance. Tall black lampposts capped with eagles reaching their wings toward the sky studded the long expanse of the bridge. A wide pedestrian sidewalk ran down each side of the roadway.

Halfway across I paused and looked over the bridge rail and down into Rock Creek Park. Most of the trees were bare of leaves but were so densely packed I couldn't see through them to the ground. A horse trailer with its ramp down was parked below me. A park ranger on horseback must be patrolling the trails that snaked through the park.

When I looked up to continue my walk I quickly turned my back to hide my face. Across the road, on the other pedestrian sidewalk, Mavis Forrester strode along, heading across the bridge in the opposite direction. Once she passed me I turned back around. Mavis marched more than walked, eyes straight ahead, with her shoulder bag gripped in one hand. She wore her mink with a cashmere scarf wrapped loosely around her neck. She didn't see me, and I didn't hail her. Instead I wondered what on earth she was doing this far northwest. She was blocks away from her apartment and even further away from the Library of Congress.

Instinct told me not to let her spot me, so in case she looked back I turned back to the bridge railing and grabbed on to a streetlight, leaning over as if watching something down below. After a minute I glanced back at her. She was already across the bridge and on the street, still walking quickly and purpose-fully. My training spoke to me and I went after her, thinking I'd tail her until she got to her destination. I was curious about her. After all, she'd been in the bar when Floyd Stinson's corpse was found, too.

I walked as quickly as I could, but my stride was no match for hers. I was going to lose her, damn it, and I couldn't break into a run without attracting attention. Mavis stopped in the middle of the sidewalk and jaywalked across the street toward Al Becker's building. Could she possibly be visiting Al? And if Mavis knew Al, what did that mean? Might she have known Floyd Stinson too?

Mavis didn't go in the front door to the apartment house, but quickened her pace as she went around the building. I followed her, half running now because she could no longer see me. As I rounded the side of the building I didn't see her anywhere. I grabbed at the handle to the back door of Al's building, but it was locked. I kicked it in frustration, and then looked up the street. I didn't know for sure if she'd gone inside, for just on the other side of the building a maze of streets stretched away in several directions. She could have vanished from sight among them.

In frustration I pulled on the door handle again, then, fuming over losing Mavis, I trudged back toward the bridge and crossed over it. While waiting for my bus I found a pay phone and called Sergeant Royal.

We met for dinner at a mom-and-pop Chinese restaurant off Virginia Avenue near George Washington University. Sergeant Royal lowered himself into his chair, wincing as his knee joints bent. The waiter came over with his pad. 'Double bourbon on the rocks, Jim Beam,' Royal said.

'I'll have a martini,' I said. 'No olive. Practically no vermouth. And separate checks, please.'

Royal grinned at me. 'We're going dutch? You're a modern girl, then?'

'Mostly,' I answered. 'Besides, I called you and asked you to meet me.'

'Damn good idea, too,' he said, spreading his napkin over his lap and tucking it into his belt. He looked suspiciously at the menu.

'I've never had Chinese food before,' he said. 'I have a feeling I'm not going to like it.'

'Let me order for you,' I said. 'You'll enjoy it, I promise.'

The waiter dropped off our drinks and asked for our order.

'Chinese fried chicken with mashed potatoes and green beans for the gentleman,' I said. 'I'll have egg foo yung. And egg rolls to start for both of us.'

'I hope you have something useful to report after your afternoon with Al Becker,' Royal said after the waiter had left our table. 'I'm stymied.'

'Sergeant Royal,' I began.

He put a finger to his lips. 'Call me Harvey. Surely we know each other well enough. Besides, I'd just as soon not tip off anyone here that I'm a policeman.'

'OK. Harvey. I guess I want you to know that I think Al is innocent of the murder.'

'Based on what?'

'He told me all about his past, about working for the German embassy, about knowing Floyd Stinson for years, everything he'd hidden from you. He said he just didn't think, that he was afraid you'd suspect him. He told me that he was going to find you and tell you everything in the morning.'

'Did he now? Well, let's see if he turns up.'

Our waiter interrupted us with the egg rolls.

'Do I have to eat one of these?' Royal asked.

'Yes.' I picked one up, dipped it in sauce and crunched into it. Royal, eyeing his roll dubiously, followed suit.

'This is OK,' he said. 'Sort of like fried cabbage. Now tell me why you think Stinson is innocent.'

'The man has lived here for years. He's a US citizen. He loves his work – you should have seen the pleasure he took in giving me a tour of the zoo. He's being treated badly by old friends because he's German. And he just accepts it.'

'That's sweet, Louise, but it's meaningless.'

'What facts do you have that implicate him? That he knew Stinson for years? Does that mean he murdered him?'

'It doesn't. But Al is the only one of the folks in the bar that knew Stinson.'

'Why are you limiting your suspects to the bar customers? We're just witnesses to the discovery of the body. Cal was the only one who knew for sure the body was behind the bar.'

'My dear girl,' he said, 'any one of the customers could have come in the back door before the place opened, murdered Stinson, dragged him behind the bar, run off, then come back later to see what had happened after the bar opened.'

'Oh,' I said.

'Do you remember how cold it was? The street was deserted. We canvased the neighborhood and no one saw anyone suspicious. Or Cal could have let the murderer in. Or left the door unlocked. That boy doesn't have much between his ears.'

The waiter arrived with our meals. After his first reluctant bite of his Chinese fried chicken, Royal dug in and ate every bit of it.

'This tastes like no fried chicken I've ever had,' he said. 'What are these flavors?'

'I don't know them all, but garlic, I'm sure, Chinese five spice, soy sauce and lots more. Want to taste my egg foo yung?'

'No thanks. I like my eggs for breakfast.'

After the waiter cleared our plates we both ordered coffee.

'When our dinner came I had the feeling you had more to tell me,' Royal said.

'When I was walking over the Taft Bridge I saw Mavis Forrester coming across from the other direction.'

'Really? You're sure?'

'Positive.'

'That's blocks away from her apartment.'

'I don't think she was walking for her health. She moved very purposefully.'

'Did you see where she went?'

'No. The first thing I did was turn my back to her so she wouldn't recognize me. But I waited too long to start tailing her. I couldn't catch up to her.'

'You don't think she was going to see Al Becker!'

'I wondered that too. But she didn't go in the main door of his building, she went around the corner. By the time I got there she was nowhere in sight. The back door to Al's building was locked. Someone could have been waiting for her and let her in, I suppose. But the streets around the building are crowded with row houses and small businesses. She could have gone into any of them.'

Royal tapped his teaspoon on the table, then pulled out his notebook and pencil. He scribbled in his notebook for a few seconds. He seemed to make some kind of decision before he spoke to me.

'About Mavis,' he said. 'The FBI check came back on her. I had assumed she must have some money of her own. You should see her apartment. But do you know, her mother was a cleaning woman! No father's name on her birth certificate. She graduated from a Catholic high school at the top of her class. She doesn't just work at the Library of Congress, either; she's the head of the circulation department. She's got top security clearance and not a blemish on her record.'

'Her salary couldn't possibly pay for that ring she's wearing.'

'I noticed that rock too. Maybe she has a sugar daddy.' Harvey suddenly blushed crimson. 'I apologize, Louise, for my language.'

'For Pete's sake, I'm not a child. I know what a sugar daddy is.'

'And the Maxwells, you should see what the FBI's got on them! My God, the entire family was in bed with the Nazis before the war. They were charter members of the German American Bund and America First. They don't have the money they used to, either. What with the Depression and all.'

'Maybe that's why Leo Maxwell wants to marry the Scott girl. She's likely to get a chunk of her husband's fortune when they divorce.'

If I was an honest woman who deserved the trust that Harvey placed in me, now was the time to tell him that Stinson worked for OSS and was ransacking the old German embassy for anything of intelligence value. Which made it very unlikely, in my opinion, that the 'suspects' drinking in the bar that night had anything to do with Stinson's death, either one of them as an individual or several of them as a group, including Al. Al was a clerk at the zoo, not a German operative. And an agent would never have returned to the scene of an operation, or be so careless as to be spotted by a bystander.

We beckoned to a waitress for refills, but she shook her head. 'Sorry,' she said, 'we're out of today's coffee ration.'

Out on the sidewalk we stood stamping our feet and pulling on gloves.

'Let me give you a ride,' Royal said. 'It's still awfully cold out.'

I didn't want him to know I was spending another night at OSS. He didn't know what branch I'd transferred to and I wanted to keep it that way.

'I can catch a bus,' I said. 'There'll be one right along.'

'OK,' he said, 'if you say so.' He turned up his collar and limped across the street to his beat-up woody. I headed for the corner and the bus stop.

The bus driver must have seen me coming because he waited for me, idling the big blue-and-white rig. There wasn't another soul on board. Maybe he just wanted company.

When the door opened I had my foot on the first step when I recognized the driver.

'Hey there,' Walt said. 'I didn't know you were so friendly with that policeman. Did you have dinner together and chat about the murder?'

I'd passed my limited spycraft course with flying colors, and my instructor would have approved of me. I didn't miss a beat, just kept climbing up the steps.

'I just ran into him,' I said. 'We were friends before what happened at the Baron Steuben. Besides, what business is it of yours?'

Walt turned to me. He hadn't shaved today and his eyes were bleary. I hoped he hadn't been drinking. I slid into the seat at the front of the bus and directly across the aisle from the driver. I wanted to keep an eye on Walt. If he looked shaky at all I was getting off this bus. There were no other passengers, and I figured his guard was down.

'Sorry, sister,' he said, 'you're right, it ain't my business. Most everything's not my business. I just drive a bus. I'm not the kind of person who gets to know things.'

Walt revved the bus, as if it was a sports car, and we peeled away from the bus stop.

'Slow down,' I said. 'You've been drinking.'

'It's just you and me. I could drive this route blindfolded with one hand behind my back. I've been doing this for years. Besides, Capital Transit would never fire me. There aren't enough drivers as it is and they ain't going to hire colored men.'

But Walt did slow down. We passed by the Baron Steuben Inn. The neon martini sign was lit, so it must be open. Cars were parked outside up and down both sides of the street.

'Cal could charge admission, if he wanted to, for a tour of the back of his bar,' Walt said. 'The place is packed every night now. The last time Chippy and I stopped by Cal asked us to sit at the bar and keep our regular table open for bigger spenders. It's the story of my life: "Get out of the way, Walt, you're nobody."'

I recognized the Maxwell mansion as we passed it. The upper floors were dark, but the ground-floor windows leaked light around the blackout curtains. Walt slowed down and gestured toward it as we passed it.

'You remember the rich guy from the bar? That's his place. Or rather his daddy's. Before the war this whole block full of mansions, including the German embassy, would be lit up like Christmas trees. You could hear bands playing inside, see men and women in tuxedos and evening dresses on the patios. All their servants used to ride my bus. You should have heard the stories they told!'

Walt pulled to a stop at a bus stop where no one was waiting. He reached under his seat and pulled out a bottle of Four Roses. 'I got my one bottle of whiskey for the week today,' he said, waving it around.

'Stop it, Walt,' I said.

'Or what?' he answered. 'I told you Capital Transit will never fire me. I know how much I can drink and still steer this jalopy.' But he didn't take a drink from the bottle, stuffing it back under his seat. 'You know which one of these mansions is the German embassy?' he asked.

'Yeah.'

'It's got seventy rooms in it. Seventy! Thirty bedrooms! And we got army guys guarding it. And the Swiss are taking good care of it. What kind of sense does that make? We should grab it and sell everything in it.'

'It's against international law.'

'Did you know that there's millions of dollars in there somewhere? The Germans used it to pay off their spies and informers.'

'I heard that. It's just another Washington rumor.' We were still idling at the curb. 'Walt, shouldn't we be moving?'

'Oh yeah,' he said, shifting his gears. The bus shot away from the curb.

'Cut it out!'

'You see any other vehicles? Calm down, you're safe with me.'

I calculated the earliest stop I could get off this bus. I didn't want to freeze, but I didn't want to die wrapped around a streetlamp, either.

The conference room in Que building was wonderfully warm, heated by the camp stove in the corner, lit by the glow of its coal fire. I counted three other female bodies on cots, and another empty cot for me. I just took off my shoes, coat and scarf and slid under my blanket. I didn't want to wake anyone.

'Glad to see you,' Miss Osborne whispered to me from the next cot.

'I hope I didn't wake you!'

'Not at all. I was wondering if I should send out an arctic patrol with a dog sled to look for you.'

'Sorry! I had dinner with Sergeant Royal.'

'If you didn't learn anything critical let's talk about it in the morning.'

That was fine with me. I was bone-tired, cold and frustrated. I think I fell asleep before my head even touched the pillow.

SEVEN

'Are the eggs hot?' Merle asked me.

'I would say lukewarm,' I answered. 'And powdered. But the bacon is good. And there's strawberry jam for the toast.'

'There seemed to be a full complement of cooks in the kitchen this morning, thank God,' Miss Osborne said. 'The food has been so awful the last couple of days.'

The OSS cafeteria was about half-full of people chattering and reading newspapers while they ate breakfast. The flu crisis must be waning. Maybe we'd be able to sleep in our own beds tonight. Even better, the temperature was above freezing. We could see people on the streets again. And the zoo animals would venture outside their animal houses. Remembering the zoo made me think about Al and his sad situation. He was a murder suspect only because he was a German by birth and he knew the victim. Lying to conceal his background only worsened his situation.

'Miss Osborne,' I said, as the three of us bused our table, 'I need to brief you soon about the project we've been working on. I have a concern we need to talk about.'

'Of course,' she said. 'Merle, will you finish the sample card this morning while I talk with Louise?'

'Sure,' he said.

'I thought that was done yesterday,' I said.

'We'll talk about it when Merle is finished,' she answered.

Miss Osborne's office was as small as mine, but it was wallpapered with maps of Europe stuck full of pins and samples of the black propaganda we'd produced in the few months since the Morale Operations branch had been established. It was an impressive display, but I knew it would be nothing compared to what we would need to do to camouflage the coming invasion. I figured we'd be spending lots of nights at the office, and not due to the weather.

Miss Osborne sat behind her desk and leaned back in her chair. 'Fill me in,' she said.

I told her everything that had happened since I last briefed her.

'Does Royal have any thought that Stinson was more than a custodian?' she asked. 'That he might be working for one of the clandestine services?'

'Not that I know of,' I said. 'He hasn't said anything to me.'

'Good. And the FBI isn't involved in the investigation?'

'They've run background checks at Sergeant Royal's request, but that's all.'

'Good, excellent,' Miss Osborne said, nodding her approval.

'But ma'am,' I said, 'I'm becoming concerned about something.'

'Just spit it out.'

'By not telling Sergeant Royal that Stinson worked for us and that the murder might be related to espionage we're running the risk that Stinson's murder might never be solved. And it throws suspicion on people who could be innocent. Royal suspects that Al Becker killed Stinson. Just because Al knew Stinson personally, they worked at the German embassy together years ago, and because Al didn't tell him the truth about his past. And there's no connection between Stinson and the others at the bar.'

'Why does the murderer have to be one of the people at the bar?'

'Because the streets were deserted due to the cold. Neighbors didn't see anyone else in the area. Royal thinks Al murdered Stinson in the storeroom and hid the body behind the bar. He came back to the bar as a customer later to see what had happened. And because he was supposed to meet Stinson to play chess and the regular customers would wonder where he was. The bartender hadn't called the police yet because he was terrified.'

'You don't think Al Becker killed Stinson, then.'

'No, ma'am, I don't. Just because he was born in Germany and knew Stinson, that's not motive or evidence.'

'I'm sorry, Louise, I can't permit you to tell Sergeant

Royal about Stinson's work for us. There's no way a police officer can be counted on to keep information like that confidential.'

'But an innocent man might be arrested for murder!'

'This is war. One person's fate isn't important enough to warrant jeopardizing our operation. When the publicity over Stinson's murder dies down we are going to try to recruit one of the Swiss caretakers to take over Stinson's work looking for intelligence.'

'Are you sure there aren't millions of dollars hidden in the embassy?'

Miss Osborne shrugged. 'Of course there's no money in the embassy. Why would the Germans keep cash there? They had bank accounts just like everyone else.'

Just because I didn't smoke didn't mean I couldn't take a mid-morning break. I waited for Sergeant Royal on the corner of Virginia and 'E', two blocks away from the OSS campus behind the War Department. It was a spycraft given that a crowd was the best place for a private meeting. Here there were so many knots of military men, secretaries taking their cigarette breaks and men in trench coats looking enigmatic that we would be completely invisible. Just another couple standing outside having a private conversation on a cigarette break.

I was still bundled up against the cold but the sun was shining full force down on me, and it felt good.

A police car, with Dickenson at the wheel, pulled up next to me. Harvey got out of the passenger side and Dickenson drove off. Harvey limped up to me.

'I've got maybe ten minutes,' I said.

'This won't take that long.' Royal looked furious. The frown lines had deepened around his mouth and eyes.

'What's happened?'

'When I got to Becker's apartment this morning he was gone.' He lit a cigarette, cupping his lighter against the wind.

'What do you mean, gone?'

'He took a bunk, Louise. I listened to your instincts instead of my own. I didn't put a watch on Al Becker, and now he's escaped. He's had all night to get away and we have no idea where he went.'

I was dumbfounded. And embarrassed. I'd believed so completely that Al was innocent. Was it because I felt sorry for him? If so I wasn't anywhere near as competent as I thought I was. I'd fallen for his pitch, that he'd been badly treated because he was German born and that being considered as a murder suspect was just more of the same sort of prejudice. I couldn't believe I'd been so naive. Had I learned so little in two years in Washington?

'I don't know what to say.'

'Louise, I know you meant well. You're so capable most of the time that I forget you're a girl. You're going to be emotional when you like someone. I should have remembered that.'

I felt the heat rise in my face and deep in my coat pockets I clenched my fists. I clamped down on my feelings; damn it, I wasn't going to act like a girl and cry now. Royal didn't seem to notice my distress.

'When Dickenson and I got to the apartment Becker didn't answer the door. So I found the super and got him to unlock it. Becker's clothes and private items were gone. There wasn't a scrap of paper, an old toothbrush, not even yesterday's newspaper, in the place. I'm telling you he stripped the place like an expert.'

'He had a fancy car. Easily identifiable.'

'It was still in its parking spot, stripped clean too. Becker must have abandoned it because it would stick out like a sore thumb on the road. Why drive when he could catch a train at Union Station in the middle of the night and go anywhere in the country?'

'I'm sorry,' I said, and then immediately regretted it. Men never apologized, so why did I feel like I had to?

'Louise, because we're friends, because I've admired your past work, I shared what I knew about this case with you. You haven't kept anything from me, have you?'

Yes, actually, I have. I haven't told you critical information about the murder victim: that he worked for OSS, and that his assignment was to search for intelligence documents in the German embassy. And that his murder might have something to do with his mission. And that if Al was his murderer, he might be a spy, too. And I'm hiding this from you only because OSS doesn't want the FBI to find out that OSS is intruding on their territory. Which they would if you informed them that espionage could be behind Floyd Stinson's murder.

As badly as I had messed this up, I still knew when to keep my mouth shut.

'Harvey, I swear what I told you was the truth,' I said. My lies weren't blatant, I told myself. I just hadn't told him everything I knew.

'OK,' he said. 'I'll take your word for it.' My stomach cramped painfully again, but I forced my face to stay relaxed.

'Good. I need to get back to work,' I said.

'Me, too.' He dropped his cigarette butt to the sidewalk and ground it out with the sole of his shoe. He gestured for Dickenson, who'd parked across the street, to pick him up. I turned and walked east back to the OSS compound. When I got there I'd have the pleasant task of telling Miss Osborne that I'd been wrong about Al Becker. At least I could assure her that Sergeant Royal was still unaware that Floyd Stinson was an OSS operative.

It didn't matter one bit to Miss Osborne that I had been wrong about Al Becker. Or that Sergeant Royal was angry with me.

'As long as your sergeant doesn't find out Floyd Stinson worked for us, you've done your job,' she said. 'That's all that matters.'

Not to me, I wanted to say. I needed to know why Al Becker murdered his 'friend' Floyd Stinson. Was it personal? Did it have something to do with Stinson's work for OSS? With the years they worked together at the German embassy? When I saw Mavis Forrester on the Taft Bridge, was she on her way to see Al? If so, why? And it still bothered me, like an unscratched itch, that Leo Maxwell and Gloria Scott had chosen the unremarkable Baron Steuben Inn to meet in for a drink. If they didn't want to be seen in public, why not get the butler in Maxwell's pile to fix them one? I bet the Maxwell liquor cabinet contained more than one bottle of whiskey. Unless Al was found and tried, or Royal unearthed new evidence and readmitted me to his confidence, I would likely never know. I hated feeling that my work was unfinished. And Stinson's murder still felt like part of my job. Which Miss Osborne had made clear was no longer the case.

'Louise, dear,' Miss Osborne said. 'Please pay attention.'

With disbelief I realized that Miss Osborne had been speaking to me and I hadn't been listening!

'I'm so sorry, ma'am,' I said.

'I understand that the Stinson murder is on your mind,' she said. 'But that's over for you now. We have other work to do.'

'Yes, ma'am.' I was mortified. For the second time today I'd been reprimanded by someone whose opinion of me I cared about very much. I needed to pull myself together before I completely lost my reputation for competence.

I pulled my heavy cardigan around my shoulders. It was cold in Miss Osborne's office, but not as cold as it had been. We didn't need to wear coats, and Miss Osborne had discarded her *ushanka* and substituted a scarf wrapped loosely around her neck. We'd turned the conference room back to its original purpose and been told we could go home tonight. Our adventure in holding down the fort was over, at least until the next bout of bitter weather or flu epidemic.

Miss Osborne and I were in her office and glad of the privacy. I took out my notebook and pencil and waited for her instructions. She pulled a sheet of paper out of a file folder and handed it to me.

'Merle's rendering of Krampus,' she said.

It was perfect. Brilliant, in fact. Merle had spent so much time recently forging German materials I'd almost forgotten he was an artist. The creature that leaped out from his drawing would give anyone nightmares, even someone not familiar with the Krampus legend. The black, hairy creature lunged at me off the drawing paper. His back legs, one human and one cloven, propelled him forward. Glaring eyes, a long red pointed tongue and dirty sharp teeth filled his face. Enormous goat horns crowned his head. He brandished a whip in one hand and gripped a basket in the other. A basket to transport people into Hell.

'It's wonderful,' I said. 'Perfect. Has Merle laid out the card yet?'

'The drawing is astonishingly good, yes. But I'm afraid the Planning Committee has rejected it.'

'What?' I said, taken completely by surprise for the second time that day.

'General Donovan felt, and so did the rest of the members, that using a fairy tale character on the card would not be effective.'

'Krampus is not just any fairy tale character. He's, well, ancient. Historic. A part of every German's childhood nightmares.'

'I know, Louise.' Miss Osborne's all-business expression was replaced with a look of sympathy. 'I understand. I explained all that. I liked your concept myself, or I wouldn't have presented it. The committee wants something, well, less . . .'

'Creative.'

She smiled at me. 'I'm afraid so.'

'Do we need to look for another idea?'

'The Committee has taken care of that for us.' She pulled another sheet of paper out of the folder. 'This will be the background to the card, in a shadowed grey, with the same words, "The worst is yet to come", superimposed in heavy black.'

The background was just a jumble of Allied flags. I didn't see the point to it. I was pretty sure the German people were already acquainted with their enemies' flags.

'This is it?'

'Yes.'

I wanted to ball up the artwork and throw it across the room, but instead I handed the paper back to her.

'Merle said you could keep his drawing of Krampus if you liked.'

I would like. I tucked it into my bag.

'Now,' Miss Osborne said. 'Time to move on.'

On the way to lunch I stopped at Merle's office, retrieved the drawing from my bag and knocked on his door. He called out to me to come in. He was at his drawing board as usual, the heels of his cowboy boots hooked over the bars of his stool, his walls crowded with samples and alphabet charts and sketches. He noticed the Krampus drawing in my hand.

'You got the bad news, then,' he said.

'Yes, indeed I did.'

'Fools. Bureaucrats should manage and let us think and create,' he said. 'What a waste.'

I held the paper out to him. 'Would you sign and date this for me?'

He grinned and took it from me, signing it in ink with a flourish.

'This is the first original work of art I've ever owned,' I said. 'Really, Merle, it's great.'

'Thanks,' he said. 'I worked hard on it. Less on the flags.'

Back in my own office I carefully pinned Krampus to the wall where I could see him from my desk. I was in the mood to be leered at. It was only lunchtime and I'd already been humiliated twice.

I opened the door to 'Two Trees' with relief. I'd come to think of it as home, and I was glad to be home. Away from my failures for a night, anyway. I dumped my valise on the floor and hung up my coat, hat and scarf on the already overloaded coatrack. The odor of Dellaphine's fried chicken drifted down the hall toward me. We had her fried chicken once a week, but I never tired of it. Especially if it was served with mashed potatoes and green beans cooked with fatback. Yes, with the coming of the war Washington, DC had become a cosmopolitan city and world capital, but in some ways it was still a Southern town.

Phoebe came out of the lounge to greet me. She wore one of her pretty caftans and her hair had been freshly washed and pin-curled.

'Phoebe!' I said. 'I'm so glad to see you up and about!'

'Thank you, I feel much better. So does Ada. She's gone to work tonight.' Phoebe took me by the hand and drew me toward the lounge. 'Come and have a drink with Henry and Milt and me. We're toasting my good health.'

I would much rather have gone up to my room and collapsed on my bed and fixed myself a martini from the gin and vermouth I hid in my pajama drawer but I couldn't say no to Phoebe. So I settled on the davenport and drew my feet up under me, first kicking off my shoes.

'So you're back from your adventures,' Henry said, sipping from a highball glass. A bottle of Jack sat on the cocktail table in front of him. Things had sure changed around here, I thought. When I'd first arrived we weren't permitted to drink in the lounge unless Phoebe suggested it, usually on Friday nights, but now the men had a drink whenever they wanted one. Milt had a highball glass in his one hand, too. Phoebe still frowned on Ada and me drinking at will, but Ada mostly went out to imbibe and I had my stash in my bedroom.

'Let me get you a sherry,' Phoebe said to me, pouring from a cut-glass-and-sterling sherry decanter into a tiny stemmed glass. I'd rather have had an inch of Henry's Jack, but there were some allowances I had to make for Phoebe's feelings.

'Sleeping on a cot in my office isn't what I'd call an adventure,' I said, answering Henry.

'What would you call it, then?' Henry asked.

'It was more like a girl scout camping trip,' I said.

'I still think it's highly inappropriate,' Phoebe said, handing me my tiny glass of sherry. I took it from her and sipped from it in what I trusted was a ladylike fashion.

'Mother, really,' Milt said. 'You're so old-fashioned. Louise has a job to do, and she can take care of herself.'

'We were well chaperoned, I assure you,' I said.

'Warm too, I hope,' Henry said.

'Very.'

'I still believe that a single woman must be careful of her reputation,' Phoebe said. 'It's one thing that will never change, I don't care what the ladies' magazines or the government say.'

I was trying to think of a reply when Milt set his glass noisily down on the table, as if he wanted us to notice that he didn't refill it. When he'd first returned from the Pacific without his left arm he drank quite a lot. He seemed to have accepted his disability now and wanted us to know it. Washington was full of men who were much worse off than Milt; you saw men in wheelchairs and blind men learning to walk with white canes on the streets every day.

'Oh, Joe telephoned earlier today,' Phoebe said, her worries about me subdued for a while.

I felt my gut contract. Why would Joe be calling the boarding house in the middle of the day?

'Really?' Henry asked. 'What did he want?'

'He said he'd be out of town for work for quite a while and didn't want us to worry if we didn't hear from him,' she said.

'How long will he be gone?' I asked, hoping no one would notice the quaver in my voice.

'He didn't say.'

'Did he say where he was going?' Henry asked.

'Of course not,' Phoebe answered. 'No one tells anyone anything anymore. Everything is top, top secret.'

'I can't imagine why a university lecturer would leave town in the middle of a college semester,' Milt said. 'It makes no sense. I wonder what the man actually does.'

I leaped in to protect Joe's cover. 'You know, if the military needs someone to teach a language somewhere they'd pull a lecturer from the university if they needed to.'

'I suppose so,' Milt said, picking up the evening paper.

Dellaphine's scrumptious fried chicken settled like rocks in my stomach. I was so worried about Joe it was all I could do to conceal my feelings, much less eat. Where could he be headed? He worked for the Joint Distribution Committee, a Jewish charity, now working covertly to help Jewish refugees escape occupied Europe. Teaching Slavic languages was his cover. He could be on his way back to New York, or on a flight to Lisbon, Geneva, even Algiers. Anywhere Jews fleeing the Nazi regime might congregate. Maybe he'd been assigned to a permanent job overseas. Depending on his mission I might not hear from him for months. For a second I didn't think I could bear it and almost burst into tears. But crying was something a modern girl wasn't supposed to do these days.

'Are you all right, Louise? You haven't eaten much,' Phoebe said.

'I'm fine. I ate lunch late,' I said, folding my napkin neatly next to my plate so I could use it again at our next meal.

Phoebe and I cleared the table and took the dishes into the kitchen, where Dellaphine's brown hands were already submerged in hot water and suds scrubbing the pots and pans.

I grabbed a dishcloth and lifted a skillet from the drain board to dry it. Phoebe left to join the men in the lounge. At last I allowed hot tears to surge down my cheeks. It was impossible to hide my feelings from Dellaphine anyway. She was the one person in the house who knew how I cared about Joe.

'What is it, baby?' she said, still scrubbing the dishes. 'What's wrong?'

'Joe,' I said. 'He's gone, maybe for a long time, and I have no idea where.'

Dellaphine nodded. 'I know, Miss Phoebe told me. Mens be doing that a lot these days.'

'He didn't call me or leave me a letter or anything.'

'Mr Joe would have told you if he could.'

'He could be in awful danger.' Like millions of others, I thought. Except for those of us here on the United States mainland. I mean, we all carefully blacked out our homes at night, the Civil Air Patrol watched the skies like hawks, and on all our coasts private boat owners patrolled the seas. But everyone knew our country was safe. There was no way the Germans had the resources to get anything but a few submarines, which they could no longer spare, across the Atlantic. They didn't have even one aircraft carrier! The Japs might have bombed Pearl Harbor, but an amphibious landing on the west coast was beyond their resources. When a reporter asked Admiral King what he'd do if the Japanese came ashore in Oregon, he cracked, 'Get the Oregon Highway Patrol to arrest them.'

No, here at home our main worry, apart from the safety of loved ones overseas, was the discomfort of rationing. More Americans were working and making good money than in a generation. Girls had good jobs, even colored girls like Madeleine. Even women with children went out to a job every day! I fretted about what would happen after the war when the men came home. Would there still be good jobs for someone like me? Or would I need to go husband hunting?

By the time I was done drying the dishes my head was pounding so hard I couldn't think. I went up to my bedroom to take some aspirin and sponge off my face. There was no way I could join the others in the lounge and pretend to be

interested in the news. As if mirroring my feelings, the
weather was worsening again. The thermometer outside
Phoebe's kitchen door registered at sixteen degrees. An awful
storm was brewing in the Atlantic and the entire country was
worried about the President again. The USS *Iowa* should be
approaching the eastern coast by now. Surely a battleship as
new as the *Iowa* could ride out a winter storm, even a bad
one, couldn't it?

I couldn't possibly go to sleep yet.

Back downstairs in the hall I swathed myself in my coat
and scarf before peeking into the lounge.

'Louise,' Phoebe said, spotting me in the doorway. 'Where
are you going?'

'Out for a walk. And I may stop for a drink somewhere.
I'm terribly restless. Don't wait up for me.'

I was out the door before Phoebe could remind me how
inappropriate it was for me to go out for a drink at this hour
by myself. Bowing my head into the wind, I crossed
Pennsylvania Avenue to the filling station on the corner. It was
closed, but the pay telephone booth next to the single repair
bay glowed dimly. I closed the door behind me and picked up
the receiver, depositing a nickel and dialing Joe's apartment.
His roommate, Ken, answered the telephone.

'I thought you'd call, Louise,' he said. 'Joe wanted to talk
to you before he left but he knew you were at work and he
just didn't have time.'

So Joe had thought about me. I grabbed on to that thought
and clung to it.

'What can you tell me?' I asked.

'Dearie, I don't know anything myself. I don't know where
Joe's gone or how long he'll be gone. He did give me his
share of two months' rent in advance, but said he didn't know
about after that.'

'What luggage did he take?'

'His big suitcase, a carpetbag and his briefcase.' That awful
scratched-up ancient leather briefcase he carried around. I'd
thought of getting him a new one for Christmas before
I'd settled on a fountain pen.

'He must be going overseas, then. Lisbon, maybe?'

'I just don't know,' Ken said. 'Don't assume the worst. He might not even leave the country.'

'If you hear from him, will you let me know?'

'Of course.' There was no 'of course' about it. Only if Joe told him to call me would I hear from Ken. It all depended on Joe's assignment.

'Thanks,' I said.

'Try not to worry.'

I hung up the receiver and left the booth. The last thing I wanted to do was go home. I wanted a drink. A cold martini, not a warm one from the bottle of gin stashed in my room. Just then a bus drew up to the bus stop a few feet from the telephone booth and idled. The driver looked at me expectantly. He must have thought I was waiting for him. I noticed the destination sign read 'Massachusetts Ave' and I thought of the Baron Steuben Inn. It was meant to be. I'd return to the scene of Floyd Stinson's murder for my martini. It would take my mind off Joe.

The Baron Steuben was exactly as I remembered it, except that tonight it was packed with customers despite the cold weather. A middle-aged man with his sleeves rolled up was behind the counter with Cal. The owner, maybe? Capitalizing on the bar's notoriety? Every stool at the bar was taken and every table occupied. It looked as if I'd have to stand to drink my martini. Then I spotted Mavis Forrester's ash-blond hair. She sat at her usual table near the blazing fire with her book and a drink, but this time the drink was whiskey, not coffee. The bar must have gotten its ration. I caught her eye. For a few seconds I swear she cast her eye around the room, as if hoping there was somewhere else I could sit, but then she gave in and beckoned me over.

'Returning to the scene of the crime?' Mavis asked.

'I suppose. I wanted a drink and was nearby.'

Cal came up to our table. Notoriety suited him. He looked almost healthy, very thin but without the dark circles under his eyes and the sheen of sweat above his lip I remembered.

'Mrs Pearlie?' he said. 'It's nice to see you again. What can I get you?'

'Martini, with a dash of vermouth, no olive,' I said.

'And you, Miss Forrester? A refill?'

'Please,' Mavis said, pushing her glass across the table toward him. 'Jack Daniel's.'

Cal picked it up with a flourish and went back to the bar.

'He looks much better than the last time I saw him,' I said.

'It's shocking that he wasn't arrested for not reporting Floyd Stinson's corpse as soon as he saw it,' Mavis said. 'You're pals with that policeman, Royal. You should know why he wasn't.'

'Cal was so terrified, and the sergeant felt he wasn't strong enough to stab Stinson so deeply.'

Mavis unsnapped the clasp of her pocketbook and pulled out a pack of Luckies and a cigarette lighter, gold by the looks of it. 'Want a cigarette?' she asked.

'No thanks, I don't smoke.'

She shrugged and lit hers, inhaling deeply. Mavis was dressed casually, in the same corduroy slacks and fisherman's sweater she wore when I'd first met her. But she still wore the diamond and ruby ring I'd noticed earlier. It was some ring. I wondered where she'd gotten it. She wouldn't have inherited it from her mother, a cleaning woman. Maybe she did have a sugar daddy, as Harvey Royal had suggested.

Cal brought us our drinks. I sipped my martini. It wasn't the best one I'd ever had, but it would do.

'So,' Mavis said, flicking her cigarette ash on the floor. 'Just how cozy are you and Sergeant Royal?'

'Cozy is not the word I would use. We're friends.'

'How did you get to be friends with a worn-out cop? I wouldn't think he'd be part of your set.'

Curious as I was about Mavis, I found myself getting increasingly annoyed at her attitude.

'What's that supposed to mean?' I asked. 'If you must know we met several months ago. How is none of your business.'

She raised her eyebrows and nodded slightly. 'You're pricklier than I thought. OK, truce. Did you hear that Al Becker ran for the hills? Do you think he killed Stinson?'

'I know Al ran.'

'Did that surprise you?'

'Yes. I liked him. I didn't think he had anything to do with the murder. I guess I was wrong.' It was all I could do not to ask Mavis if she was visiting Al the evening I passed her walking on the Taft Bridge.

'Al did have an innocent, simple demeanor.'

'Did you know him?'

'Not well. Just from seeing him here in the bar. Oh, and I ran into him on the street a couple of times. His building is not far from a restaurant where I often meet friends. The restaurant's around the corner from the Wardman Park Hotel. Al lived in an apartment building across the street.'

I clutched my martini glass stem so hard I was afraid I might have cracked it. To hide my response I took a sip from it.

'Across the Taft Bridge?' I asked. 'That's quite a way from here.'

She shrugged. 'It's the Bistro Français,' she said. 'Have you heard of it? It's worth the bus ride. There's no veal these days, of course, but the coq au vin and the onion soup are delicious.'

Right then I knew I'd be searching out the Bistro Français as soon as I could. If she dined there as often as she said, then the staff should remember if she'd been there yesterday evening after I saw her walking across the Taft Bridge on my way back from Al's. That would answer my question why she was in his neighborhood, so far from her apartment. Oh, I'd accepted that Al had murdered Floyd Stinson. Otherwise why would he have run off? But finding where Mavis was headed that night would end any speculation that she was involved.

For a few minutes we sat in silence, sipping on our drinks, while Mavis finished her cigarette. She smoked it down to the filter before dropping it on the floor with the other one and crushing it with her foot. I almost made a snarky remark about her carelessness with floors that were not her own, but didn't want to antagonize her. The woman interested me. She'd been so unmoved when Stinson's body had been found behind the bar Saturday night. And she was oddly unconcerned with what anyone thought of her.

'Want another?' she asked, eyeing my empty martini glass. 'It's on me.'

'Sure,' I said, curious why she was asking. I'd have thought she'd want me to leave so she could get back to her book.

Mavis raised her empty glass and caught Cal's eye, and nodded toward me also. This would be at least her third drink, which seemed like too many on a weeknight, especially for someone as reserved as she was.

'Since you and Sergeant Royal are such great pals, I guess he told you about my past. He ran a background check on all of us, you know. Since I work for the government, like you, my life story is in my personnel file for the police to see.'

I was surprised she'd bring up that topic. 'What?'

'You heard me.'

Cal brought us our drinks. After he left the table she leaned toward me, her perfect hair swinging forward, hiding her face. 'If you tell anyone, anyone at all, about my family, or rather my lack of a decent one, you'll regret it,' she said. Then she leaned back in her chair and lit another cigarette.

I decided not to lie to her. I figured she would know if I did.

'I would never reveal any information given to me in confidence,' I said, 'about anyone. Ever.' I wanted to tell her it was my job to keep secrets, but couldn't, of course.

'So you know my mother was a cleaning lady and that I'm fatherless. I wouldn't want that to get out; people still care about such things. I have a good job and respectable friends and I don't want them to know.'

'Of course. I understand completely.'

'How could you know what it is like to grow up on the very bottom rung of society? To live in one room in an alley tenement? I got a scholarship to a Catholic high school and spent all four years alone. No friends. No invitations to dances or birthday parties. It gave me plenty of time to study, though, and I graduated valedictorian. That offended everyone, including the teachers, but they could hardly deny it to me. And then I got a good job at the Library of Congress. Good enough so I could forget where I came from. Then the war came. Bad luck for the men who left to be cannon fodder, good luck for me. I kept getting promoted to take their places. And I have a regular civil service position, not a contract for the duration. I'll keep my job even when the men come back.'

'I do understand,' I said. 'My family owns a fish camp in coastal North Carolina. I worked there every weekend and summer during school and again after my husband died. It took an hour-long bath and a lot of cologne to erase the smell of fish from my body. I went to junior college because a great aunt left me enough money for tuition, but I only had one real friend there. She was Jewish, so we were both outsiders.' Unlike Mavis, my contract was for the duration of the war. I didn't want to lose my job after the war. I envied Mavis' civil service job.

Mavis inclined her head slightly, as though giving me some credit for my working-class upbringing.

We were interrupted by a man with a drink who stopped by our table. He was presentable, dressed in a decent suit and I guessed about fifty.

'Girls,' he said, 'there aren't any stools at the bar, and I wondered if I could join you?'

Mavis didn't even pretend to be polite.

'No,' she said, 'you cannot. But you can borrow this chair and take it somewhere else.' She lifted her coat from the empty chair sitting between us and shoved it toward him. The man, completely nonplussed, just stared at her, then moved away in search of more amiable companions, dragging the borrowed chair behind him.

'You don't mince words,' I said to Mavis.

She shrugged. 'Why bother? He's a nobody.'

We sipped our drinks. 'You know,' she said, 'I remember once when I had to go to work with my mother. Her boss, the housekeeper, insisted that I sit in a chair in the kitchen the entire day. I was seven. I had to ask the housekeeper's permission to use the bathroom. I was a reader even then, so I had a library copy of *Doctor Dolittle* with me. No one believed I could read it until I read a few paragraphs out loud to them.'

Mavis stuffed her book into her pocketbook and picked up her mink.

'I need to go,' she said. 'Work tomorrow.'

She casually strolled through the bar, turning quite a few heads despite her age.

I still had most of my second martini to drink, but I noticed a party of four standing up near the door, right where cold air would be blasting at them, staring at me. I could take a hint. I left the table to them and went over to the bar, where I was able to grab an empty stool.

'Want me to top off your drink?' Cal asked, as he wiped down the counter.

'No thanks, two is my limit. I'll just finish this one.'

'I saw you talking with the ice queen,' Cal said.

'You mean Mavis? She is a bit glacial.' I reminded myself of her background. I expected she had to be tough as an old boot to pull herself up from her origins the way she did. 'How often does she come in here?'

'Oh, a couple of times a week. She likes to sit by the fire. She's not my favorite customer. She never tips, and she always grinds her cigarettes out on the floor so that I have to clean them up. She tells me I need to remember to leave ashtrays on all the tables, and I do. I can't help it if the patrons move them around. I mean, she could grab one from another table, couldn't she? I think she enjoys watching me mop.'

Cal's boss called out to him and he went to the other end of the bar. The man who'd asked to join Mavis and me at our table seized that chance to edge up to the bar beside me to try his luck again. 'Miss,' he said, 'can I buy you another drink?'

'No thank you,' I said. 'I'm just finishing this one and then heading home. Work tomorrow.' Really, since coming to Washington I'd gotten more attention from men than I thought possible. At thirty I was no longer young, either. But Washington was full of young and not-so-young unattached men – and girls, for that matter – eager to have fun, away from home and the watchfulness of families, neighbors and church. Who would know if they drank and stayed out all night? But the social scene was booby-trapped, for girls anyway, by damaged reputations, unwanted pregnancies and venereal disease. Girls could still be 'ruined' for life.

'Perhaps I could drive you home?' my would-be suitor asked me. At least he was polite and not standing too close to me.

'No thank you,' I said. 'I'm not interested.' He gave up with grace, shrugging and turning around to lean on the bar.

'OK,' he said. 'I get it.' He sipped on his drink. 'Do you come here often?' he asked me, but in a purely conversational tone this time.

'No, this is just my second time.'

'It's always full of Germans,' he said. 'You know when the German embassy was open this was its local bar. Not for the big shots, you know, but for the rest of them. And for German-Americans, too. They served German beers and liquor, schnapps and such. All that changed when the war came. Some guy who worked at the embassy before the war was murdered here a few nights ago. Makes you wonder.' My new acquaintance drained his glass, set it down on the counter and drew on his coat. 'Nice to meet you,' he said. I nodded back at him and he was gone.

Yes, it did make me wonder. Just how much Floyd Stinson's murder had to do with his job at the German embassy. And if Al Becker killed him, did that have something to do with his years at the embassy? Or Stinson's work for OSS? I thought again about Harvey Royal's theory that someone in the bar that night was the actual murderer. A customer who killed Stinson in the storeroom, then came into the bar afterwards to see what Cal did when he found the body. And stayed to see what happened. If this was true, then didn't either the killer or Stinson need to have a key to the back door to get inside the bar before it opened? And why were they meeting in the bar's storeroom?

'Cal!' I called out to the barkeep. Cal got to me after depositing two beers on the counter for other customers first.

'Change your mind about that drink, ma'am?' he asked.

'No, but I do have a question for you. How many people have keys to the back door of this place?' I leaned my chin on my hand and waited.

Cal blanched. 'Just me,' he said. 'And the boss.'

'Really? That's all? This place has been around for years. Are you sure?'

That scared rabbit look that Cal had the night of the murder returned. Sweat beaded on his forehead and grey shadows gathered around his eyes.

'Please, ma'am!'

'Tell me. I won't tell anyone, even the sergeant.' I'd already lied to Harvey once, what was another one?

'OK,' Cal said, lowering his voice. 'There's one on the ledge outside over the back door. I put it there in case I forgot mine. The boss would fire me if he knew.'

'Anyone else know about that key?'

'I didn't tell anyone.'

I removed my chin from my hand. 'It's OK,' I said. 'Go on back to work.'

Cal scurried down the length of the bar. So he kept a spare key above the back door. And where did anyone look for a spare key? Above the door. And I remembered what Sergeant Royal had told me. That we didn't know for sure what happened here before Joe and I walked in that night.

Outside on the sidewalk I stared at the black hulk of the old German embassy across the street. The moon was waning, but it still shed some decent light. On a street full of opulent mansions, including the Maxwells', the embassy's only dramatic architectural quality was its size. I decided I would call it 'Victorian ugly'. The façade was flat and unrelieved except for a mansard roof and a small tower. Large square windows, without any adornment, stared blankly out at the world. The building rose up for three tall stories not counting the basement. I'd heard it had seventy rooms, so it had to extend back for many feet. Even the door was unpretentious. It was blocked from my view by an ordinary squat brick portico, built to shelter cars that pulled up to the front door.

The embassy seemed vulnerable to me. Two soldiers with war dogs were assigned to guard it twenty-four hours a day, but I saw no sign of them tonight. Perhaps it was simply too cold to post anyone outdoors. I knew from Miss Osborne that a Swiss caretaker lived in the building, but I saw no lights on the second floor, which I assumed held all the bedrooms. I wondered that it was so unprotected. It must be full of expensive furniture, art and even personal possessions left behind by the German occupants after they were rounded up and detained in Virginia. And the third floor, again according to

Miss Osborne, was rumored to be the prewar headquarters for the Nazi espionage network in the United States. It was the US Army's responsibility, and the Swiss legation's, to see that the embassy was undisturbed until after the war. The same procedure protected our empty embassies in the Axis nations and occupied countries.

Despite having downed two martinis after a tough day I was wide awake and had no desire to go home. My worries about Joe resurfaced and caused my chest to contract and my heart to pound. I wondered when I would hear from him, or see him again. The amount of luggage he took with him meant to me that he expected to be gone a long time. If he was on his way to Lisbon, or another neutral city in Europe, I might not see him until the end of the war, if then. I knew this could happen. It was one reason we didn't discuss marriage.

My life would have been so much easier if I'd fallen for some 4-F government bureaucrat!

I still saw no army patrol in front of the embassy. My curiosity overwhelmed me, and I walked across the street and right up to the building's portico without anyone hailing me. Three more steps and I was at the double mahogany door. Just because I could, I grasped the fist-sized doorknob and tried to turn it. Of course the door was locked.

I went down the steps and around the side of the building and found a narrow veranda decorated with reproduction classic urns full of dead plants. Two leaded glass doors led inside from the veranda, both locked. Curtains were pulled over the doors and I couldn't see inside.

Still no guard. I would circle the building, and if I didn't find a soldier and a dog on my walk I'd tell Miss Osborne tomorrow, General Donovan would call the army and then there'd be hell to pay. Freezing weather or not, someone should be guarding this building.

Behind the building a short flight of steps led down to a basement door. A back drive ended there, so it must be a service entrance. Basement windows lined the rear of the house, peeking above ground level, but they were heavily barred, so at least there was some protection from entry. Overhead a fire escape descended from the roof down the rear wall, ending far over my head at a window on the second floor. I assumed that if it was needed one of those extension ladder gizmos could be dropped from the second floor to the ground.

Still no patrol. By now I'd pushed Joe's absence and Floyd Stinson's murder out of my mind and was just concerned. The German embassy appeared unguarded. I went down the stairs to the basement door and turned the doorknob. The door was unlocked. I pushed it open and saw a narrow hall leading into darkness. Quickly I closed the door again and sat down on the steps outside to think.

EIGHT

The German embassy was wide open. There was no sign of the army. The Swiss caretaker apparently forgot to lock the basement door. This would be a scandal if the newspapers got wind of it.

Of course I planned to report this to Miss Osborne in the morning. But I was fighting a powerful urge to go inside the building. There was no one to stop me. Blackout curtains at the windows blocked the view of the interior. I should be able to explore freely, on the downstairs floor anyway. And if I was spooked at all there were more than enough windows to escape through if I couldn't get to the back door.

I worked for OSS. I was practically a spy myself. Any operative worth his or her salt would take advantage of this opportunity. Who knew what I might find? As far as I knew, Stinson could only have searched the embassy during daylight hours, when the Swiss caretaker was up and about. Perhaps I could even get into the third floor!

What would Miss Osborne say? I knew her well enough to be sure that if I was successful she would think it was a grand idea. If I wasn't there would be hell to pay and I could find myself back home in Wilmington gutting fish in no time.

I stood up and brushed off my trousers. Looking around one last time, I went down the short steps, opened the door, went inside and closed the door behind me. Moonlight didn't penetrate the blackout curtains and it was dark inside. Pulling my army penlight (another souvenir of my training course) out of my purse I switched it on after clicking the red lens into position. I was in a short hall with two elevators directly ahead of me. I turned to my right and walked into a kitchen large enough to serve a hotel. It was furnished with a double range, two refrigerators and a metal sink as big as a bathtub. Pots and pans hung from ceiling fixtures. Bowls and baking dishes lined a hutch. I skirted the long wooden worktable and opened a door to find a pantry bigger than my bedroom. It was empty except for a box of toilet paper and a pile of neatly folded rags.

I crossed the hall to the other side of the building and found myself in a butler's pantry lined with cabinets and drawers. Sparkling crystal winked at me in the light of my flashlight. A set of gold-trimmed fine china filled a wall of glass-fronted cabinets. It must have had fifty place settings. I pulled out a drawer, gently, in case it squeaked. Tarnished sterling silver flatware, stamped with the pre-Nazi German imperial eagle, filled it to the rim. Several more doors opened off the room. I opened one; it appeared to be a large servant's room, probably the butler's. Another was an office crammed with several roll top desks and file cabinets. Excitedly I pulled out drawers, only to find them empty or filled with useless housekeeping records.

I went back the way I came, through the kitchen and into a long narrow hall lined with doors. I opened one on to what had to be a servant's room. It contained an iron bedstead and a small dresser. Dark wallpaper in wide stripes of burgundy and brown closed in the space and there was a tiny coal fireplace. I opened several more doors and found similar rooms, none with any personal possessions in sight.

I paused in the narrow hallway, covering my flashlight lens with one hand, and listened. I heard nothing. Training my flashlight on the floor I went further down the hall and opened a large door. I sensed rather than saw a massive space beyond me.

Taking a deep breath I shone the full light of the flashlight ahead of me into a huge, elegant room. The ceiling must have been thirty feet high, the walls sheathed in dove-grey silk. Three heavy chandeliers overhead, now wrapped in sheets, would have lit the room for receptions and parties. I could hear tiny tinkles coming from the crystal drops as the fixtures swayed slightly overhead. Above a set of tall mahogany double doors maybe twenty feet high perched a gilt eagle, its wings stretched over the door lintel, its talons clutching a swastika. An oversized red-and-black Nazi flag, which hung from the ceiling to the chair rail, dominated another wall.

The room was decorated in a more modern style than the servants' quarters. I sat down on a curved, sleek davenport upholstered in maroon raw silk and covered my flashlight lens again.

This was the embassy drawing room, where the German ambassador would have welcomed guests from all over Washington and the world. I saw oil paintings stacked one on top of the other against the walls and occasional tables crowded with objets d'art. Crystal decanters, highball glasses and tumblers filled a bar counter in a corner.

As a working-class American girl I felt overwhelmed by the abundance of it all. I'd once been to a party at Evalyn McLean's mansion, but this felt different. McLean's house was lavish, but this was decadent.

I waited for my nerves to settle while I decided whether I was going to continue to search. I was no longer sure why I was here. I was stunned by how unguarded all this opulence appeared to be. I still heard nothing, just the tinkle of the chandelier crystals overhead as the fixtures swayed.

On the cocktail table in front of me a group of miniature silver and ivory clowns pranced. They were exquisite. One in particular attracted me. The little clown wore a silver top hat on his ivory painted head and held a real lace parasol overhead. He had one foot on the ground and the other raised a bit, as if taking a step. Under his other silver arm he carried an ivory ball. His tiny collar was made of lace too. He was so precious I had to restrain myself from picking him up.

My God, there was a gold cigarette lighter the size of a deck of cards resting on the cocktail table next to an inlaid cigarette box. Surely it wasn't solid gold? I hefted it. It could be, it was heavy enough. Think of how much it was worth! I set it back down on the table.

Since all the windows were hung with closed blackout curtains I decided to continue my progress through the rooms downstairs. I appeared to be completely alone. If anyone was spending the night in the house he was probably in a second-floor bedroom and as long as I was careful and didn't trip over a silk ottoman he wouldn't hear me.

So I went on through the double doors guarded by the Nazi

eagle and into the front foyer. It was just as overwhelming as the drawing room. A black marble mosaic of a swastika was embedded into the center of a Carrara marble floor. I skirted around it as I went into the next room, the library.

Hundreds of books filled the built-in bookcases, which were carved with pillars and lintels to look as if they were freestanding. Two delicate writing desks with pens, inkwells and stationery at the ready stood under windows. An overstuffed sofa and several club chairs suitable for reading completed the furniture arrangement. I went over to a display case that contained what appeared to be antique books. I reached in and took out a small leather bound volume. I couldn't read the title, but the author was Friedrich Nietzsche. His signature was scrawled below his name on the title page.

By the time I found the dining room I was so repulsed by the excess of my surroundings I just glanced at the long dining room table with chairs lined up like soldiers, another gilt-and-crystal chandelier the size of an armchair and several sideboards crammed with sterling silver. I felt almost dizzy from the emotional impact of being inside this place and imagining what had gone on here. I leaned against the back of a chair to regain my composure.

Then I heard it. A tiny sound, way too much like the noise of a squeaky door opening and closing a few rooms away for my liking. I froze in place, my grip on the back of the chair tightening, ready to pick the chair up and fling it at anyone who found me. Every sense I had, especially my hearing, focused on the distant spot where I'd heard that sound.

I'd been a fool to come inside the embassy. I was too tired, and had drunk too many martinis, to make a sensible decision. After I'd found the back door unlocked I should have made my way home and told Miss Osborne in the morning. And let the Swiss, the army and the FBI handle the problem. If I got caught in here I would be their problem!

Then I heard the sound again. Nearby this time. Definitely the noise of a swinging door on hinges being quietly pushed open, then slowly closing. Sweat trailed down my backbone. I had both hands on the chair now, ready to lift it over my head.

There were two entrances to the dining room. One set of French doors from the hallway that stood open and one leading from what I suspected was a butler's pantry, where the servants would organize platters and such before bringing them in to serve guests. I heard a tiny scraping sound at the pantry's swinging door, saw it move slightly and then settle back. Another tiny scratching sound, the door opened again and a calico cat pushed through. When he saw me his tail jerked straight up into the air and he crouched as if to pounce on me, his fur standing on end. I have never felt such relief, setting down the chair and almost falling into it. I'd been terrorized by a watch cat patrolling for mice!

I wanted out of this nasty place as soon as possible.

I walked quickly, or as quickly as limited light and caution would allow, back through the house into the kitchen area. I reached for the back doorknob and turned it. The door was locked.

I tried the lock again. It was definitely engaged. After my initial shock I told myself that there was a reasonable explanation. The Swiss caretaker, who I'd begun to picture in my mind as a blond, three hundred pound man in a nightshirt, had come down in the elevator to check the doors and finally locked this one. The man would be back in bed by now.

Thank God I'd been so quiet. Thank God I'd used the red lens on my flashlight. Thank God I hadn't interrupted the caretaker while he was downstairs. Thank God the cat was just a cat.

But now what? How was I going to get out of here?

I wandered back into the vast drawing room to sit on the davenport and think. I found tears welling up in my eyes, why I couldn't exactly say. I found myself wondering how much of this display of wealth was stolen from people the Nazis had persecuted. And I thought of all the influential Americans, like the Maxwells and Henry Ford, wooed here at glittering parties by the German ambassador. And how close I'd come to being discovered.

But before I even started to plan my escape my eyes fell on the cocktail table and I noticed the prancing clowns had been rearranged. Not just rearranged. One was missing. The one I'd admired so, the one with the lace parasol and the ivory ball. And the heavy gold cigarette lighter was gone too.

In the time it had taken me to explore the foyer, library and dining room someone had stolen them. And it wouldn't be the caretaker. Or the cat.

I'd been trained to prepare for the worst-case scenario. Which, in this case, was that I'd interrupted someone in the process of burglarizing the embassy, someone with a key, who'd entered before I arrived and left before I returned, locking the door behind him. Someone who'd been nearby the entire time I'd been inside the embassy. Or maybe he had simply locked the door and was waiting for me around a corner?

Then I did something they didn't teach me at The Farm. I would have run away, but there wasn't anywhere to go, so I hid. I found a closet, with coats still hanging, and curled up inside. Slumped right down to the floor with my back to the wall, I drew my knees up and wrapped my arms around them while I tried to compose myself. I recognized the telltale signs of panic. Ringing in my ears, a pounding heartbeat, sweat trickling down my backbone and spots in front of my eyes.

Then my training kicked in and I remembered my instructor at The Farm. I had to force myself to take deep, slow breaths while counting. By the time I'd counted to twenty-five I was able to think rationally. I figured the intruder was gone. Surely he wouldn't want to encounter me any more than I wanted to meet him. The last thing either of us wanted was to rouse the caretaker, who wouldn't hesitate to call the police. He was probably armed, too.

Who would have a key to this embassy? The Swiss were supposed to control the building.

The custodian! Of course, the custodian would have keys! Floyd Stinson, who'd been the custodian here since 1931. Whom the Swiss had kept on. Who'd known Al Becker for years. That must have been Al's motive! Al had murdered Floyd for his keys to the embassy and had been pilfering from it ever since. Including tonight. But Al had left town. Hadn't he? Was he here tonight?

Had he left the embassy and locked the door behind him?
Or was he still inside?

I don't know how much time passed before I suppressed
the physical symptoms of fear and could focus on what I
needed to do. I had to get out of this building. It shouldn't be
difficult, I told myself. The basement windows were barred,
but the main-floor windows weren't. I would climb out one
of them.

I left the coat closet and flicked on my torch, again using
the red lens. I went through the kitchen and into the first servant's room I came to. Edging around the bed in the tiny space
I found the window lock and unlatched it. Grabbing the lower
sash I shoved upward. The window didn't budge. It must not
have been opened in years. I put my full weight into my next
shove. The window creaked and shuddered but still didn't
open. It must be painted shut, damn it!

I moved out of that room and went into the next. When I
tried to open its window the same thing happened. The window
simply wouldn't shift. Taking a chance, I trained the flashlight
beam on the window and inspected it. The window had been
nailed shut.

After trying a dozen windows on the ground floor, one after
the other, I gave up. The embassy wasn't as vulnerable as I
thought. With the basement windows barred and the ground-
floor windows nailed shut, the building was impregnable so
long as all the heavy doors were locked. The second floor, the
bedroom floor, was many feet above ground and besides,
the custodian slept upstairs every night. No wonder the army
only posted two guards with dogs and withdrew them when
the weather was frigid!

I was trapped inside the embassy. It would be amusing if
it wasn't so serious. I didn't think that the Swiss legation
would appreciate it much if an OSS employee was found here,
sleeping on a davenport in the drawing room, in the morning.

I was less afraid than I was when I first discovered the back
door locked. It seemed to me that whoever had been inside
the embassy with me, who'd stolen the items from the drawing
room, had locked the door behind him when he left. If it was
Al, as I thought it must be, there was no good reason for him

to stay behind and confront me. He was wanted for murder. He'd want to escape and avoid me, so no one would know he was still around. He certainly wouldn't want to dispose of my body!

I had to get out of this place myself. I wondered if my Schrade switchblade could pry out the nails from one of the smaller windows in a servant's room. But that would leave marks that might be found and signal that someone had been in the building. I considered hiding until daylight, hoping that someone would open up the place, the Swiss guardian would leave for the day and I'd have an opportunity to escape. Even if I did, in daylight someone might see me.

My only option left was the fire escape.

The window where I'd seen the first escape route to the fire escape was on the second floor. I'd have to go up to the bedroom floor and hope I didn't disturb the sleeping Swiss caretaker. I now pictured him as carrying a handie-talkie with a direct line to the FBI and armed with a Furrer submachine gun. I hoped he was a heavy sleeper.

I took off my shoes and stuck them in my pocketbook. Staying close to the wall to avoid squeaks, I slipped up to the head of the stairs without revealing myself, to be brought up sharp by Adolf Hitler's face staring down at me! I gasped and dropped my flashlight before I realized I was looking at a portrait. I froze, hoping the caretaker hadn't heard me.

But I heard distant snoring, so the watchman must be asleep. And I was grateful that the sound was on the other side of the house, away from the fire escape.

Tiptoeing down the hall to the back bedrooms I counted doors and windows until I thought I had found the correct room. Gently I opened the door. I was correct. I could see the metal work of the fire escape at one of the room's windows. I went inside and carefully closed the door, leaning against it in relief when the latch clicked softly shut.

This room was quite modern. A large bed stood against a wall paneled in leather. A luxurious art deco wool rug in abstract grey and black covered the floor. A black Barcelona chair sat next to a cocktail table covered with magazines. And in the corner rested a shiny chrome-and-porcelain bathtub large enough for two people. I wondered if this had been the ambassador's room. Or perhaps an impressive guest room for important visitors from the Reich?

I padded across the rug to the window, shoved my flashlight into my bag and grabbed the lower window sash. To my intense relief I raised the window with no trouble. Climbing out on to the steel balcony, I turned around and closed the window behind me. I had escaped, and relief flooded over me. If only I wasn't twenty feet off the ground!

In the light of the waning moon I still saw no one patrolling the grounds.

The hinge of the movable ladder that I needed to release to reach the ground had rusted. I had to work on it for a few minutes with my knife before it would move. Jiggling the ladder gently, I was pleased not to hear a lot of noise. So I lowered it carefully to the ground and climbed down. When I reached the bottom I put my shoes back on and ran. I moved as quickly and quietly as I could, eager to get away from that shut-up building, like a raccoon that had worked its way out of a trap.

Without looking where I was going I plunged on to the sidewalk on Massachusetts Avenue and smack into Leo Maxwell. I almost didn't recognize him. A scarf wrapped around his hat and neck concealed part of his face. He grabbed at me to prevent me from tripping over his feet.

'Mrs Pearlie! What in God's name!' he said, keeping a hand gripped around one of my arms. I pulled away from him.

'I was just out walking,' I said, lying like a professional. 'Through the back gardens at the Lutheran church.'

'Dear, you were running like a maniac. And it's late. Shouldn't a working girl like you be home in bed?'

The best lie is the one that is mostly true. 'I had a couple of drinks at the Baron Steuben,' I said. 'Then I took a walk to clear my head. And I saw something move. It startled me so I ran toward the street. It was probably a cat.'

'You came out of the alley beside the German embassy,' he said. He pulled a pack of cigarettes out of his pocket, shook one loose and lit it. He seemed intent on having a conversation and I wanted to avoid one at all cost.

'Is it against the law to use the alley to get to Massachusetts Avenue from "N" Street?'

'Of course not,' he said.

'Why are you out here, anyway?'

He grinned at me, blowing smoke and frozen breath into the space between us.

'I live just a few houses down the street,' he said, 'and I never go to bed until after midnight. I often take a late walk.'

'It is late, and I do need to go,' I said, buttoning my heavy coat and winding my scarf, which had come loose during my flight, close around my neck and face.

'Look, my car is parked on the street in front of my house. Let me drive you home.'

'That's not necessary,' I said. 'I can get home on my own.'

'Don't be a little fool,' he said, taking my arm again. 'It's late at night and freezing, and you're alone. And you said yourself you've been drinking. Anything could happen. Let me run you home. Where do you live?'

I pulled my arm away from him again, but he was right. I was cold and exhausted. I had no idea if I could find a taxi at this hour.

'Near Washington Circle,' I said. 'And thanks. I guess I could use a lift.'

It didn't occur to me until we were inside Maxwell's expensive but aging vehicle that he could have been the person who was inside the German embassy with me. Maybe he had a tiny silver clown and a gold cigarette lighter stashed in his coat pockets. If his family needed money as much as I thought they did, and he was as familiar with the building as he'd implied, burglarizing the embassy made some sense. Did he have a key to the back door? If he'd been in the embassy with me, had he seen me? Did he leave the building before me, locking the back door after him? Was it a coincidence that he was waiting on the sidewalk for me when I ran into the street?

I stared at Maxwell's handsome profile as he pulled away from the curb, shifted gears and headed down the street. God help me if Maxwell was the burglar and had seen me! He could be taking me anywhere. Somewhere lonely, where he could strangle me and dump my body, leaving him free to loot the German embassy at will.

'What are you snickering about?' Leo asked.

'I've been reading too many Agatha Christies,' I said.

Of course Leo Maxwell drove me straight home. Our trek through the dark, empty Washington streets was uneventful. We talked about who in our households had been sick, when President Roosevelt would be back in the country and whether the whiskey ration would be lifted soon.

When we stopped outside 'Two Trees' Maxwell turned off his car's engine. 'Mrs Pearlie,' he said.

'Yes?' I wasn't paying close attention to him. I was as tired as I had been in my life. I just wanted to crawl into my bed with a hot-water bottle. Morning would come way too soon to suit me.

'I was wondering, would you like to have dinner with me sometime?'

Exhaustion must be causing me to hallucinate, I thought.

'What?'

'Dinner. Could we have dinner together? Maybe this weekend?'

How ludicrous! Me, an aging government girl who grew up at a North Carolina fish camp, going out with a playboy like Leo Maxwell? I knew what this was about. He wanted to pump me about what I knew about Floyd Stinson's murder.

'Aren't you engaged to Gloria Scott?'

Maxwell fiddled with the gear stick. 'Not formally. I mean, she's still married. She's in Chicago for a couple of weeks. It's just dinner.'

How could I pass up the opportunity to pump Maxwell about that infamous night at the Baron Steuben Inn myself?

'Sure, why not,' I said. I scribbled my phone number on the matchbook cover he handed me.

I practically fell into the hallway of 'Two Trees'. I was so tired my bones and muscles ached for relief. Phoebe appeared out of the lounge in a heavy bathrobe with her face framed in pin curls.

'Louise!' she said. 'I've been so worried. Where have you been all this time?'

'You wouldn't believe,' I answered.

'Louise!' I awoke from a dream in which I spent hours crossing and recrossing the Taft Bridge to find Miss Osborne standing over me. Despite three cups of strong coffee I'd fallen asleep at my desk with my head pillowed on a stack of paper. I was horrified that Miss Osborne had found me like this.

'Ma'am,' I said. 'I am so sorry! It's no excuse, but I was out late last night. I need to tell you what happened. It has to do with Floyd Stinson's murder.'

'So tell me,' she said, dropping a stack of file folders on my desk so she could stand with her arms crossed and look severe. 'You've been quite distracted lately.'

'You might want to sit down,' I said.

She sat, crossing her thin legs and resting her chin on one hand. 'Make it snappy,' she said. 'I don't have a lot of time.'

I told her everything that had happened to me since I'd last seen her, except for the part about Joe leaving town, of course. My conversation with Mavis at the Baron Steuben, my escapade in the German embassy, my theory that Floyd Stinson had been murdered for his keys to the embassy and that Al Becker might be using those keys to steal from the embassy, my narrow escape and encounter with Leo Maxwell. I concluded with Maxwell's invitation to dinner.

Miss Osborne didn't seem in a big hurry after all. She uncrossed her legs and leaned toward me, with her hands flat on my desktop.

'Good work, Louise,' she said. 'Excellent work!'

'Thank you,' I said.

'Especially since you didn't get caught. If you had been you'd be in the DC jail this morning and we'd have to pretend we didn't know you.' She grinned at me when she said that, but I knew it was the truth.

'What should I do now? Should I tell Sergeant Royal my theory about the keys?'

'I don't know,' she said. 'It would be fortuitous for OSS if Stinson's murder was solved without involving us, without anyone knowing Stinson was one of our operatives. Very fortuitous. But I must talk to General Donovan first; this is too complex to make a snap decision about. We must consider the reaction of the Swiss legation, too. They'll be answerable to the Germans for allowing the embassy to be penetrated, and I expect their reaction will be most unpleasant.'

She stood up and smoothed down her skirt. 'And as for you, Louise, I want you to take the rest of the day off. You're no good to me in such an exhausted state.'

'But Miss Osborne, there's so much to do!'

'You heard me, go home. By tomorrow General Donovan and I will have discussed all this and I will give you your instructions.'

I had no intention of going back to 'Two Trees'. Although the prospect of a nap was inviting I rarely had time off during the week, and I wanted to answer a question that had been niggling me since I saw Mavis Forrester crossing the Taft Bridge. She'd told me she was on her way to meet friends for dinner. I wanted to know for sure that was true. Yes, Harvey Royal was right and I was wrong. Al murdered Floyd Stinson for his keys. I needed to inform Sergeant Royal about this, but when I spoke to him I wanted to be able to tell him whether Mavis' story about the day I saw her on the bridge was true.

I got off the bus on the south side of the Taft Bridge. I wanted to cross it the way Mavis had to get to the restaurant, and see if that lined up with my observation at the time. Besides, I liked walking across the Taft Bridge. The view was gorgeous, even in the winter, to the north part of Rock Creek Park where the zoo was located, to the south into an overgrown wooded section of the park. I leaned over the rail briefly and noticed, as on the last occasion I was here, a Park Service horse van on the shoulder of the road that followed the creek. The rear gate was down. I assumed, as before, that a park ranger was patrolling the area on horseback. There wouldn't be another good way to cover much of the area.

Before I set off I looked up the address of the Bistro Français. It was on Woodley Road, which ran behind the apartments that made up part of the Wardman Park Hotel. Although the

weather wasn't as frigid as it had been the last time I crossed
the bridge it was still very cold. I leaned into the wind and
held on to my hat as I soldiered across the street.

As I reached the spot where I had lost sight of Mavis, I
realized that she'd bypassed the shortest route to the restaurant,
going down Calvert toward Al's building instead of up
Connecticut. I felt a rush of energy. Had she been lying, then?
But when I turned the corner past the apartment building, I
realized that I couldn't see what direction she'd been going
in. So I went toward Woodley, and sure enough there was the
Bistro Français on the corner.

The restaurant was open and packed with the lunch crowd.

A tiny maître d', bald with a tonsure like a monk's, was
dressed in a tuxedo despite the time of day. He bowed to me
at the entrance, menu in hand.

'*Madame*,' he said, 'can I show you a table?'

Why not? I hadn't had lunch yet and I was famished. Besides,
if I was a paying customer maybe he would be willing to
answer my prying questions about his clientele.

'*Mais oui*,' I said, in my schoolgirl French.

He answered me in a stream of rapid French that I couldn't
follow. He must have been able to tell this from my expression, so he switched to English.

'I hope *madame* is hungry,' he said, taking my coat, hat
and scarf from me and hanging them on a nearby coatrack.

'Always,' I said.

He showed me to a table for one nestled in the bay window
that looked out on to the street and brought me a menu, a
glass of water and a half-loaf of crusty French bread accompanied by a large pat of butter stamped with a fleur-de-lis. I
guessed that French restaurants got extra butter rations.

As I cast my eye down the menu I saw my bank account
shriveling. To pay for this meal I'd have to forgo buying a
war bond this month. Which made me wonder if someone
bought Mavis' meals here or if she paid for them herself.

There was no beef or veal on the menu. I detested most
fish and we had chicken all the time at home, so I selected
grilled lamb with *compote de pommes*. Just when I'd decided,
a waiter, whose embroidered nametag read 'Benny', appeared

to take my order. When he spoke to me his Georgia twang about knocked me over.

'Ma'am,' he said, 'what a good choice. So few people order lamb, the chef loves to prepare it. What wine would you like to have with it?'

Wine? In the middle of the day? Well, why not? One glass couldn't hurt. As long as I was here I might as well enjoy myself.

'A glass of the house white wine, please,' I said.

I tucked into the warm French bread and used up every smidgen of butter. Although thinking of things French made me wonder about Rachel, my French Jewish friend who'd found refuge in Malta when the Nazis occupied Vichy France and her husband joined the resistance. I liked to think that I had something to do with her escape from Marseille, but I couldn't be sure. What I did know, thanks to her letters, was that she and her two children were safe on Malta. With the Allies now in Sicily and southern Italy, Malta was spared constant bombardment. Food was more plentiful, and Rachel wrote that she even had a job in the dispensary at the RAF base. Her landlady kept her children during the day. It wasn't the life Rachel had expected, but she was grateful for it. One of my fantasies was that I would be able to visit her, in a liberated France, after the war. I would give anything to see her face and hear her voice again.

The maître d' interrupted my reverie when he brought me the wine. He cradled it in a starched white napkin and presented it to me. I was surprised to see a California label. He noticed my expression.

'Yes, *madame*,' he said, 'our house wines are from California or New York. Shipments from France have been disrupted, as you can imagine. But this is a French varietal grape, and I think you will like it.' He poured a swallow into my wine glass and I sipped it.

'It's quite good,' I said. He filled my glass, then held out the bottle.

'Is *madame* sure she will not want more?' he said. 'You can take an unfinished bottle home with you.'

'I'm fine, thank you,' I said. He bowed and retreated gracefully.

The waiter brought me my lunch and I tucked into it. How, I wondered, can the French cook something as simple as lamb chops with stewed apples and do it so much better than anyone else?

When I finished the waiter whisked my plate away after I declined dessert. After a decent interval the maître d' appeared at my table with the bill.

'I hope your meal was pleasing, *madame*,' he said.

'It was,' I said, and then craftily laid my trap. 'My friend Mavis told me about this place. She said your food was wonderful, and she was right.'

'Ah, do you mean Miss Forrester?'

'Yes, Mavis Forrester.'

'She dines with us often.'

'How often?'

He looked taken aback, but I gave him as charming a smile as I could manage, considering I didn't practice charming very often.

'Several times a month,' he said.

'She has quite a circle of gay friends.'

'Yes, she does. Her table is often as many as eight.'

I began to rummage in my purse for the money to pay my check. Thank goodness I kept a large bill folded up for emergencies or I would have had to spend the afternoon in the kitchen washing dishes.

'She was here on Tuesday night, I think?' I said.

The maître d' touched his forefinger to his chin, thinking. 'Yes, yes she was,' he said. 'But with a smaller party. They were four. They all ordered the lobster thermidor.'

NINE

So Mavis had been telling the truth. When I spotted her on my return from Al's apartment she was on her way to meet some of her friends at the Bistro Français. I was glad I'd checked her story. Mavis was not a person whose word I felt comfortable accepting at face value.

I strolled across the Taft Bridge. Now that the thrill of my adventure at the restaurant was over I felt my lack of sleep sapping my energy. I couldn't go home and nap yet, though. I had to contact Sergeant Royal and tell him what I'd learned, or deduced, inside the German embassy. That Al had killed Floyd Stinson for his keys to the embassy, and might still be in the city taking advantage of them to pilfer the building. If he had left town, then someone else must be stealing from it. Someone who was in the embassy with me last night. I hoped whoever it was hadn't seen me or recognized me. Which was one more good reason to talk to Sergeant Royal as soon as possible. The sooner I shared this information the safer I'd be.

The afternoon sun warmed the air a bit, so I unwrapped my scarf and lifted my face to the bright blue sky. Turning, I leaned out over the bridge rail and down into the thick growth of Rock Creek Park. The trees stretched upward, but the bridge was so far above the ground none of them reached me. Some were bare-branched, others evergreen. I spotted some kind of utility shed and a narrow trail which connected to the road that followed Rock Creek. The horse van was still pulled up on the shoulder, its gate down. The mounted park ranger must still be patrolling the park.

An open patch in the foliage attracted my attention. It was smack in the middle of a thick stand of pine trees and seemed unnatural. I leaned forward, as far as I could with the rail just below my shoulders. Stepping on to the bottom rail I leaned further out. I could see that the patch was a hole in the foliage lined by broken branches that marked a clear path to the park floor. As if something heavy had fallen through the trees, leaving a path of destruction behind it. Fallen directly below me, as if from the bridge itself. A sack of garbage, perhaps? Curious, I peered at the spot and saw, tangled in the broken branches, what appeared to be a man's white shirt.

I whipped around and ran back to the north end of the bridge, my scarf trailing behind me and my handbag bumping my hip. At the end of the bridge I saw stairs leading down to the park. I collected myself, tucking my scarf under my collar and my handbag strap over my shoulder. I started down the steps as quickly as I could, gripping the handrail. Only the fear of breaking a limb, or my head, kept me from plunging pell-mell to the ground.

When I reached the bottom of the steps I was so spent I had to lean over, breathing heavily to relieve the pain in my chest. Seeing the mounted patrolman leading his horse toward the van forced me to move before I was ready. When I got to him I grabbed his arm and spoke in gulps.

'Help me,' I said. 'Please! I saw something from the bridge. In the park. Over there.' I gestured behind me.

'Careful, ma'am,' he said. 'Don't spook the horse. Calm down. Now what did you see?' The patrolman was in his mid-thirties, I guessed, and looked much like a regular policeman in his black-belted blue wool uniform and peaked cap, except that he wore jodhpurs and riding boots. His horse was a well-settled bay, not at all bothered by me. He swished his tail and snorted foggy breath while his officer held his reins close under his bit.

'From the bridge,' I said, 'I saw a hole in the vegetation, lined with broken branches, where it looked like something large fell through. Recently. And I think I saw a man's shirt draped over a branch.'

'How do you know it's recent?' he said.

'I walked across the bridge on Tuesday,' I said. 'It wasn't there then.'

'Catch your breath,' he said. 'Can you lead me to it?'

I turned around and faced the bridge. I knew exactly where I'd been standing and where I saw the hole.

'Yes, I think so.'

'Are you afraid of horses?'

'Not at all.'

'Ride behind me, and show me where you saw the hole in the foliage. I'm Officer Weston, by the way.'

Weston mounted and reached down a hand to me.

It's a good thing I'd watched a lot of western movies. I grabbed on to his hand, stepped into his stirrup, which he'd left free for me, and hefted myself on to the horse's back behind his saddle.

'Hold on to me,' he said. 'I need both hands.'

I wrapped my arms around his waist and he nudged his mount toward the woods across the road. 'There,' I said, pointing. We plunged into the woods. If I hadn't been so fearful of what we were going to find I would have enjoyed myself. Feeling the horse's motion beneath me, hanging on to a well-muscled young man on a chilly afternoon in the park, were things I wouldn't mind doing again at another time.

But I focused on where I was going, looking up at the bridge occasionally to orient myself and pointing Officer Weston in the right direction. He actually spotted the damaged brush first.

'I see it,' he said, forcing the horse through the thick vegetation. I buried my head behind his shoulders to avoid getting scratched.

'My God,' I heard him say. 'It's a body.' He pulled the horse to a stop. 'You need to slide off first.' He handed me down and I saw the corpse. A suitcase, broken open by its impact with the ground, lay a few feet away. Its contents were scattered all around the immediate area. Weston dismounted. 'Wait here,' he said. He didn't have to tell me that. I had no intention of approaching the body. But I recognized it. It was Al Becker.

It was much colder in the shade of the park trees than in the afternoon sun on the deck of the Taft Bridge. Weston's horse nickered and pawed the ground with one hoof. I shivered as I watched the park ranger gingerly turn Al's body over.

'He's been here a couple of days, easy.'

So Al hadn't been in the embassy with me last night. And he hadn't left town, either.

'I know who he is,' I said.

Weston gave me a sharp look.

'You do?'

'Yes. He lived in the apartment building on the corner. His name is Al Becker.'

'How do you know this?'

I told him as much of my story as he needed to know. 'You'll want to call Sergeant Harvey Royal of the DC Metropolitan Police,' I said. 'He's in charge of the case.'

Officer Weston glanced down at Becker's body, then at me. 'How would you feel about keeping watch here while I go call Royal and my boss? Who knows who may have seen us come into the woods here, and I don't want any sightseers messing with the scene.'

'Sure,' I said, 'I can do that.'

Officer Weston gathered up his reins. His horse stomped and nickered, anticipating his rider mounting. 'Don't go near the body,' he said. 'A nice girl like you shouldn't see such things.'

I nodded, but clenched my fists in my pockets. I might be a girl, but I was a girl who grew up in the fishing business and I'd gutted enough fish on smelly docks slippery with blood not to be bothered by a little gore.

Weston mounted and headed down the trail we'd made searching for Becker's corpse. I figured he had a radio in the horse van so I didn't have much time. I made my way over to the broken suitcase. Its contents were strewn around the hard ground. But they'd collected dew over a couple of mornings, dampening everything, which had then acquired a thin sheen of frost. I glanced upward and saw the white shirt I'd spotted from the bridge stiffly draped over a tree branch. I crouched as far away from the mess as I could while still able to see it all.

Of course there were more clothes, frozen by frost into odd shapes. A clump of frayed boxer shorts. A pair of suspenders coiled like a snake hung over the edge of the suitcase. A Dopp kit that must contain a toothbrush, toothpaste and shaving gear had fallen close to the body. Harvey Royal had told me that Al's apartment had been stripped of personal items, and it seemed like every one of them was strewn around the forest floor. Also strewn on the grass were the picture of his wife I'd seen on my visit, a few other pictures that must have come from his bedroom, a hairbrush, notebooks and papers, one of which looked like a bank account book. A crossword puzzle dictionary and his copy of *The Ox-Bow Incident*, still bookmarked with an envelope, lay there too.

I heard the sounds of a horse's hooves returning and quickly moved over to Al's body, again crouching several feet away. There weren't many bugs – because of the cold weather, I supposed. Al's face wasn't marked, but his head was skewed at an odd angle and one arm bent unnaturally at his side and a leg folded up under his body. I was no doctor but I'd have guessed his neck, at least, was broken.

Al's death could only be a suicide or a murder. If it was a suicide it made no sense to me that he would have packed all his possessions before offing himself.

Officer Weston found me leaning up against a tree when he reappeared.

'You OK?' he asked, dismounting.

'I'm fine,' I said.

'I've called Sergeant Royal. He's on his way. And the Park Police Commandant.' Crime scene experts, photographers and a hearse would follow them, no doubt. As soon as all those vehicles appeared the usual crowd of spectators and crime reporters would show up. I'd been up most of the night, walked for blocks, hadn't had that nap, and now this. Knowing Al hadn't skipped town after all and wasn't the intruder in the embassy last night didn't help me feel any better.

'You look done in,' Officer Weston said to me. 'Sergeant Royal will want to talk to you, so I can't let you leave. But if you like you could sit in the van and get out of the cold.'

When Sergeant Royal climbed into the cab of the horse van he found me snoozing, tucked into the corner of the passenger seat covered with an army surplus blanket I'd found folded in the back.

'Louise,' he said, shaking me gently, 'wake up!'

'Don't,' I said, only half awake.

'Wake up,' he said again. 'I need to talk to you. You've been asleep here for over an hour.'

I sat up, remembered where I was and why.

'Oh God, hell and damnation,' I said, still confused with sleep. 'Al didn't skip town; someone killed him. And he's been dead too long to be the person in the German embassy with me last night.'

'What are you talking about? You're half asleep. Want some coffee? I've got a thermos.'

Then I remembered that Sergeant Royal knew nothing about my life since I had last talked to him, when he told me that Al Becker had skipped town and made me feel like a fool for believing in his innocence. If I recollected correctly, he had informed me then that since I was a girl my emotions ruled my head. I had half a mind just to keep my mouth shut and not tell him anything at all.

Royal leaned out the window of the truck cab. 'Dickenson,' he called out. 'Bring over the coffee thermos and a clean mug for Mrs Pearlie. And sugar, if we've got any left. And the bag of cookies my landlady gave me this morning.'

I changed my mind. I could be persuaded by coffee and cookies.

'I hope you've got an empty notebook,' I said to Royal. 'You're going to need it.'

'Well,' Royal said, 'goodness. You've been busy.' He flexed his fingers, aching after taking pages of notes on my story. I swallowed the last of the hot, sweet coffee Dickenson had brought me. The cookies were spice, not my favorite, but I felt better for eating them.

Of course I hadn't told Royal that Floyd Stinson worked for OSS, searching the embassy whenever he could for intelligence that might help us win the war. Royal didn't need to know any of that. I didn't lie to him; I just left out stuff and didn't answer his questions completely.

'You do realize, don't you,' he continued, 'that Al probably committed suicide. He panicked and packed to escape, but realized the futility of it and jumped off the bridge.'

'That would be the most convenient solution,' I said. 'Then you could close the case and go home and put up that bad knee and pour a bourbon.'

'That was uncalled for,' Royal said, bristling. 'And I gave you the last of my coffee, too.'

'Look,' I said, 'I've been thinking.' Royal rolled his eyes. 'It's also possible,' I said, 'that Al was murdered for the keys he stole from Stinson. Al was dead before last night, so it must have been someone else inside the embassy with me.'

'You're sure the silver clown and gold lighter were stolen last night, while you were there?' I could tell he didn't doubt me, he was just thinking out loud.

'While I was in the dining room or the library, whoever had left the door unlocked took the objects and slipped away, locking the back door behind him. But it wasn't Al. So someone else must have murdered Al for the keys he stole from Floyd Stinson. Or we could surmise that someone other than Al killed Floyd for the keys, and then Al committed suicide because he assumed no one would believe he was innocent. Which means the original killer was in the embassy with me last night.'

Royal looked at me with what could only be pity. 'Louise,' he said. 'Stinson wasn't murdered for his keys. We found them when we searched his room at his boarding house. After they were photographed and tagged we turned them over to the Swiss legation.'

I'd been wrong about everything. I was an even worse detective than I was a spy. I was so tired, and so stunned by how misguided I'd been, that I felt tears well up in my eyes.

Royal patted my arm. I wanted to draw it away, but none of this was his fault and he was trying to be kind.

'Look,' he said. 'I need to get back to work. You need sleep. I'll get Dickenson to drive you home.'

'You must have a theory about all this,' I said. 'Care to share it with me?'

'You don't know when to give up, do you? I think that Al Becker killed Floyd Stinson, that he started to leave town but instead killed himself. What happened in the embassy last night had nothing to do with it. If someone is burgling the place we need to let the Swiss legation know, keeping your name out of it, of course. I hope to God the Swiss don't call the FBI. That's all we need.' Miss Osborne and General Donovan would agree.

'But what was Al's motive?'

'I don't know. I expect it had something to do with the years they worked at the embassy together. Maybe Stinson had something on Becker and Becker killed him to shut him up. If we keep pounding the pavement and asking questions we'll find out. We always do.'

I was too tired to make small talk on the way home. Dickenson tried to start a conversation but gave up when I answered him in monosyllables.

All I could think about was Al Becker. How could I have been so wrong about him? Despite what Royal said, I wasn't convinced he killed Stinson. And why would Al have killed himself? He'd packed and was clearly on his way out of town. He had a head start. He could have caught a train at Union Station and gone anywhere in the country.

Al died the Tuesday night after I'd visited him in his apartment. I reviewed every second of that afternoon in my head. I couldn't think of anything I'd said that might have spooked him.

And worst of all, Joe was gone. This crazy night and day started when I tried to drown my thoughts of him in martinis at the Baron Steuben Inn.

By the time Dickenson parked in front of 'Two Trees' I was so shattered it was all I could do to cover the ground between the sidewalk and the front door. Inside someone had left the hall light on for me. Thank goodness Phoebe wasn't waiting up for me tonight. I couldn't cope with one of her well-intentioned lectures. Too bad she didn't know I was already a fallen woman, like Ada; then maybe she would leave me and her worries about my reputation alone.

I reached to turn out the lamp on the hall table and noticed a letter addressed to me. I didn't recognize the handwriting and there was no return address. It was postmarked 'Chicago'. I didn't know a soul in Chicago. Curious, I sat down on the hall chair and ripped it open.

It was from Joe.

I felt my heart skip a beat in my chest.

'Darling,' the letter said, 'I can't tell you where I am. I gave this note to an acquaintance to mail as he passed through Chicago. I couldn't bear to leave you without saying goodbye. I promise you I am not in a war zone and am as safe as anyone else in this terrible world can be, but I have important work to do that may take some time. I'll write again if I can. All my love, Joe.'

Relief washed over me as I slumped into the chair. Joe was not in a war zone. Which didn't exclude Lisbon or Algiers. But that was more than most mothers, wives and girlfriends could say. I'd have to be happy with that and hope that I'd hear from Joe again soon. I clutched the single sheet of paper to my heart for a few seconds before I crumpled it up and burned it in the glass ashtray on the table.

Upstairs the dark, narrow hall reminded me of my venture into the German embassy and the panic I felt when I realized I was locked inside. So I padded down the hall to Phoebe's room. Pushing open the door, I whispered to her.

'Phoebe? Phoebe? I'm sorry to wake you up.'

Phoebe sat up in her bed and rubbed her eyes. 'It's all right, dear, what is it?'

'Can I have one of your Nembutals? I don't think I can sleep tonight without one, and I'm so tired.'

'Of course, dearie. You know where they are.'

I went into the bathroom and took the tin out of the medicine cabinet. Picking a tablet out of it I swallowed it dry. By the time I returned to Phoebe's bedroom to thank her she was already curled up and snoring softly.

Milt clutched my arm with his only hand. 'The President's home,' he said. 'The USS *Potomac* docked at the Navy Yard this morning. I heard it on the news just a few minutes ago.' The *Potomac* was the presidential yacht. Roosevelt would have transferred to it from the *Iowa* in the Chesapeake Bay.

'Thank God,' I said. I felt almost as much relief to know the President was back in the country as I had when I'd read Joe's letter last night.

Milt pulled out my chair and seated me at the breakfast

table. I still felt a little woozy from the Nembutal, but last night's deep sleep and Joe's letter had returned some strength to me. Phoebe moved around the table with the coffee pot, filling everyone's cup. I slurped mine down the second it had cooled enough to drink.

Phoebe took up her seat at the head of the table and served our plates. She scooped up a helping of scrambled eggs, added two strips of bacon to the plate and passed it on to me. I added two pieces of toast smeared with margarine and tucked in, finding myself starving. I realized that I'd missed dinner last night.

'I don't know what the President thought he was doing,' Phoebe said. 'Going so far away during wartime, and with his health problems. I didn't even know where Tehran was until I looked it up in the atlas.'

'He traveled over seventeen thousand land, sea and air miles, according to the newspapers,' Henry said. 'Cairo, then Tehran, then back to Cairo. So irresponsible of him. He should have sent Cordell Hull instead. What if he'd died and we'd been left with Vice President Wallace? He's even more of a socialist than Roosevelt.'

So despite his disdain for the President even Henry was relieved he was back in the country.

'I don't understand why anyone had to go as far as Iran,' Phoebe said. 'I would think they could all have met in Cairo.'

'Because Stalin won't travel far from Russia,' Milt said.

'I guess he's a homebody,' I said.

'And Stalin won't talk to the Turks. So Churchill and Roosevelt met with the Turkish Prime Minister in Cairo and then went on to Tehran to confer with Stalin,' Milt said. 'And then they returned to Cairo to brief General Eisenhower.'

'Is there any more coffee in the pot?' I asked.

Milt picked it up and shook it. 'Some.' He leaned over and filled my cup half-full. That would have to suffice until I got to work.

Phoebe noticed me eyeing the last two pieces of bacon. 'Here, dear,' she said. 'Ada's sleeping in, so you can have hers.'

'Thanks,' I said. 'I missed dinner last night. I was so tired all I could think about was getting to bed.' I folded the bacon into another piece of toast and ate it like a sandwich.

'Speaking of food,' Phoebe said. 'Christmas will be here in ten days.'

We all groaned, knowing what was coming.

'If we want the same meals and sweets we had last year we have to hoard our butter and sugar rations. It's just not possible otherwise. So does anyone object if we don't have butter or sugar for the next two weeks?'

'I'm OK,' I said. I hated my coffee without sugar but I was willing to sacrifice for Christmas dinner.

'It's worth it,' Milt said.

'I agree,' Henry said.

'Ada doesn't eat enough meals here to really have a say. So we've decided: Dellaphine will hoard our butter and sugar rations for the next two weeks so that she can make cookies and cakes for Christmas.'

'Coconut cake!' Milt said. 'And will you make your sweet potato casserole?' he asked me.

'Sure,' I said, 'I love cooking for the holidays.'

'I'll buy the champagne,' Henry said. 'Are we asking Joe to join us for Christmas dinner again?'

'Of course, I'd planned that already,' Phoebe said. 'I'll call him today.'

I couldn't tell them that Joe had left town. They would wonder why I knew and they didn't and might guess at our relationship. Joe's roommate would break the news to Phoebe when she called.

I scooted my chair back from the table, still holding half of my bacon sandwich. 'I need to run if I'm going to catch my bus.'

'Bundle up,' Phoebe said. 'It's still freezing out!'

'The Potomac's full of ice floes,' Henry added cheerfully.

TEN

As I pulled on hat and gloves in the hall the telephone rang. I was right there so I answered it.

'May I please speak to Mrs Louise Pearlie?' asked a male voice I couldn't quite place.

'Speaking,' I said, holding the receiver to one ear while buttoning up my coat.

'This is Leo Maxwell.'

'Well, hello,' I said. Why was this man calling me?

'I wondered if you could join me for dinner tonight? Or am I too late?'

Then I remembered. After I'd escaped the German embassy I'd run into Leo Maxwell on the street. He'd driven me home and, distracted by my adventure, I'd agreed to go out with him. I didn't expect him actually to call me, especially at eight o'clock on a Friday morning.

'No, you're not too late.'

'I know you must be on your way to work. I'll pick you up at seven tonight, then. I thought we'd go to the Raleigh Hotel. Have you ever been there?'

My brain finally woke up from its Nembutal-induced lethargy. Why was Leo Maxwell asking me out on a date? He was practically engaged to a very rich socialite. I was a government girl who lived in a boarding house. I had to be at least five years older than he was. It made no sense, unless he wanted to pump me about the Stinson murder investigation. But that could work both ways. I'd have liked to know why he cared so much. I guess Harvey was right. I didn't know how to give up.

'No, but I'd love to go. I've heard how elegant it is. I'll be ready at seven.'

Merle's drawing of Krampus leered at me all day from its spot pinned to my office wall. I wished I'd never heard of the guy.

A Christmas devil watching me was exactly what I needed. Two days before, General Donovan himself had rejected Krampus after my idea for a 'black' propaganda operation in Europe. So humiliating! I hated making mistakes. And that had been just the beginning of a disastrous week.

The last few days were so crowded I wasn't sure I remembered what had happened when and where, so I went over it all in my mind. I couldn't help that Joe and I had been in the Baron Steuben Inn when Floyd Stinson's body had been found. It wasn't my fault that Harvey Royal had been in charge of the case. But once Miss Osborne told me that Floyd Stinson was an OSS operative, using his position as custodian at the empty German embassy to search it for intelligence, I should have lain very low. Instead I used my friendship with Harvey to insinuate myself into the case. And I'd lied to Royal – lies of omission, but still lies. While he trusted me completely. When given the chance I'd sneaked into the abandoned German embassy and was lucky to have gotten out without being caught. That would have been enough to get me fired. While inside I'd discovered that someone was stealing from the embassy, someone who appeared to be inside the building at the same time I was. After climbing down the fire escape I'd run into Leo Maxwell, accepted his offer of a ride home and stupidly agreed to go to dinner with him. I'd taken it upon myself to find out what Mavis Forrester was doing on the Tuesday I saw her crossing the Taft Bridge. Her 'alibi' held up. Then I came up with a theory of the case that was completely wrong. I didn't know that Floyd Stinson's keys were found in his room so I decided that he was murdered for them. I didn't know, and probably never would, who was pilfering valuables from the embassy, but there was no evidence that the person had anything to do with the Stinson murder. I'd considered Walt or Leo Maxwell as suspects, just because Walt had a chip on his shoulder and Leo lived nearby and had money problems. And I still thought they were possibilities.

I'd discovered Al's body after checking Mavis' alibi. This excluded him from being in the embassy last night but not from Stinson's murder. So confidently I'd proposed my brilliant analysis of the crime to Sergeant Royal. Perhaps Al was so despondent he had killed himself, but that wasn't proof he'd murdered Stinson. Someone else had killed Stinson for his keys to the embassy and had been in the building with me the night before. Then Harvey took pity on me and told me that Stinson's keys were found in his boarding house room when it was searched by the police, and turned over to the Swiss legation. I was mortified all over again.

After fortifying me with coffee and cookies Harvey had sent me home, cautioning me to stay out of the Stinson murder case. But had I done that? No indeed. My curiosity had driven me to accept Leo Maxwell's invitation to dinner tonight. He clearly had an ulterior motive for the invitation and I should have refused, but I was too curious about his reason for asking me. I wanted to know why.

This morning Miss Osborne had brought me a stack of files and dumped them on my desk.

'Could you go through these for me, please, Louise? They're the first reports on our Italian operation. I'd like a one-page summary of the results on Monday.'

Miss Osborne and I had worked together interviewing German prisoners of war in an effort to recruit some to take our propaganda into northern Italy. I thought we'd formed a warm relationship, but she seemed distant and preoccupied today. I hoped I hadn't lowered her estimation of me.

After Miss Osborne left I applied myself to the files. It seemed that the operation was a success. Each of the ten German POWs recruited had been dropped off by submarine, fully kitted and briefed, with a backpack full of forged letters, phoney newspapers, stencils and pamphlets to distribute behind the German lines in northern Italy. All had returned to their handlers with empty backpacks; now they'd go back into POW camps in southern Italy until the end of the war. I thought it was remarkable that none of them had tried to escape. We'd done a good job selecting them.

Each man had been debriefed on the operation and on conditions behind the German lines and I set about writing a summary for Miss Osborne.

Merle poked his head into my office. 'Lunch?' he said.

'Thanks, but I'm really not hungry.'

He leaned up against the doorjamb. 'Look, Louise,' he said, nodding at Krampus, 'he was a really good idea. The Planning Committee made a mistake rejecting it. They have no imagination at all.'

'I think he was a good idea, too,' I said. 'But it's all over.'

Merle left then, but a few minutes later he returned.

'You have to eat something,' he said. He set down a steaming cup of coffee and a plate with a slice of cake. 'One of the girls brought the cake in and I saved you a piece.'

'Thanks,' I said.

After he left I pinched off a piece of cake and tasted it. It wasn't bad for a single-layer honey cake with no frosting.

Did I dare wear this dress tonight? Ada had insisted I buy it off the sale rack at Woodies the last time we spent a Saturday afternoon shopping. I'd never have bought it on my own, but we'd had a glass of wine at the tea room during lunch before hitting the sale. I charged it, and once I got it home I regretted it. Joe and I were lucky to be able to afford a movie and a cocktail. A fried oyster dinner at Sholl's was a real splurge.

It's not that it wasn't a stunning dress. It fit me like a glove, too. Black acetate taffeta with spaghetti straps and tiny covered buttons that ranged down the bodice and ended at the point of a dropped-V waist. The skirt, gathered to the waist, dropped just below the knee. A contrasting grey-cuffed neckline matched a grey flounce on each hip embroidered with a crimson rose. The bodice was boned but I could bear it for an evening.

Why shouldn't I wear it? I was going to the Raleigh Hotel for dinner, a spot second only to the Mayflower Hotel for glamour, and I was going with a genuine playboy. One who might need to pawn some object from his mansion to pay for the dinner, but still, I was going. Luckily I had black gloves and shoes to go with the dress. The art deco lavaliere and earrings Phoebe gave me would look fine; no one would be able to tell they weren't real sapphires and diamonds. With a rhinestone clip for my hair I should be able to pass as a society girl.

I dressed and put on my usual make-up and went outside into the hall to find someone to zip me up. I heard Frank

Sinatra's voice emanating from Ada's room and knocked on her door.

'Come in,' she said.

I found her sitting on her bed painting her toenails bright red. She wore Chinese red lounging pajamas and a pink turban wrapped around her head.

'Holy smokes!' she said to me, gaping. 'You look gorgeous! I told you you'd have a chance to wear that dress. Where are you going?'

I turned my back to her so she could zip me up. 'The Raleigh Hotel.'

'No joke! That's high-class. Who are you going with?'

I didn't dare tell her that I was having dinner with Leo Maxwell. I would never hear the end of it and I didn't have a reasonable explanation for how I met him. I sure didn't want to tell her about the corpse behind the bar.

'I'm just doing escort duty. A friend of a friend needed a date. His boss asked him to a dinner and he didn't want to show up alone when everyone else had a wife or girlfriend.'

'Is he single?'

'Of course he's single. I wouldn't go out with him otherwise.'

Ada turned me around and studied my face.

'You need eyeliner.'

'No. It makes my eyes itch. Besides, it doesn't accomplish much once I put on my glasses.'

Ada had given up trying to get me not to wear my glasses on dates.

'Your lipstick is a good color for you. Just make sure to reapply it after you eat something.'

'Yes, ma'am.'

'Let me pencil in your eyebrows.'

'Ada!'

'You're mighty thin in the eyebrows.'

'Oh, all right.'

I sat on her bed while she worked on my brows. When she was done I checked my reflection in the mirror and I had to admit that I looked less like a rube than usual.

'See?' she said.

'You're right.' I plunked back down on her bed. 'Why aren't you dressed? Don't you work tonight?'

'The boilers at the Willard are low on fuel oil and they can't get a new delivery until Monday. They've shut down the ballroom and the restaurant so the guests don't freeze in their rooms.'

I went downstairs to wait in the lounge in front of the fire until Leo arrived. When Milt saw me he threw me a piercing wolf whistle. 'Louise, you're a knockout! Where are you going?'

'The Raleigh Hotel, for dinner.'

'That's a swell place.'

'New beau, dearie?' Phoebe asked, dropping her mending into her lap. 'What's his name?'

'It's a mercy date,' I said, 'with a friend who needed an escort for a dinner with his boss.' I avoided inventing a name, one of the first things I learned at The Farm during my basic OSS training.

I heard a car horn sound outside and hastened from my seat.

'Is that him?' Phoebe asked. 'Well, he has terrible manners. He should come to the door.'

'I know,' I said, and pecked her on the cheek. 'See you all later!'

I hastened outside, throwing on my coat and gloves, glad that Leo had honked for me even if I did feel summoned. I didn't want anyone to recognize him from the society pages.

Leo got out of the driver's seat and moved around the car to open the door for me.

'Good evening,' he said. 'Did I choose a cold enough night to go out? I've got the heat blasting.' He was bundled up in a black cashmere coat with a white dress scarf wrapped around his neck, his frosty breath billowing around his face.

When Leo had driven me home the other night it was too dark and I was too preoccupied to notice his car. Now I saw that it was a 'Doozy'. I was familiar with the expression, but had never seen a Duesenberg before. The jungle-green roadster was aging but elegant, the leather worn in a few places, especially on the driver's side of the bench seat. When Leo started the motor all the needles on the round dials leaped into action and the engine engaged with a contented purr.

The façade of the Raleigh Hotel reminded me of the Willard – not surprising since the same architect had rebuilt it. Faced with limestone and brick, it rose thirteen stories high. Wrought-iron balconies and a Beaux Arts tower made it the grandest of Washington's hotels until the Mayflower was built. Until the war a spotlight from the rooftop garden lit up the Washington Monument every night. For some reason I didn't know the hotel was named after Sir Walter Raleigh, who established the Roanoke Colony in my home state of North Carolina.

Leo drove up to the very front door of the hotel and parked. He tossed his keys to a colored man in hotel livery. 'Hang on to those keys,' he said. 'I've lost the other set.'

'Yes, sir,' the valet answered. 'Like they was my own baby.'

I'd never heard of valet parking until I'd come to Washington. That some people didn't even need to park their own cars was a revelation to me. Leo handed me out of the car. I felt quite grand getting out and walking under the awning on his arm, and found I was excited about the evening. Which was just what he intended, I thought to myself. I still had no idea why he'd invited me and I needed to stay alert.

The girl at the cloakroom took my blue wool coat with the fur collar which I had thought was so elegant when I bought it and hung it on a coatrack between the minks and sables already hanging there. Leo handed over his topcoat and hat. He was wearing a navy blue wool double-breasted suit with a white shirt, navy-and-yellow paisley tie and a matching handkerchief that poked out of his breast jacket pocket. His dark blond hair was slicked back with the comb marks showing.

As Leo turned to me he seemed to notice me for the first time, running his eyes down my body and back up to my face as if I was a polo pony he was considering buying. He didn't have that leer that some men have when they check out a girl's figure, but it was obvious he hadn't thought of me like that until now and was pleasantly surprised. Amazing what

a black cocktail dress off the Woodies' sale rack could do
for a girl.

'You look lovely,' he said, offering me his arm. 'Let's get
a cocktail first, shall we?'

The hotel had just been redecorated and the interior was
terribly sleek and modern. Peach-colored mirrors faced all the
old marble columns in the lobby. We walked across a black
marble floor striped with white marble. The ceiling was silver
leaf and blue, the walls paneled in teak wood. Modern Chinese
Chippendale furniture, which I recognized only because I'd
seen it in an advertisement in *Ladies' Home Journal*, finished
off the new look of the lobby.

Leo waved off a cigarette girl as we stepped up a level into
the cocktail lounge of the Pall Mall Room. Decorated in rose
and chromium hues, the lounge was even more sophisticated
than the lobby. The room wasn't crowded yet. That would
happen hours from now, when decent people were in bed, as
my mother would say. We took a spot near the small stage set
up for a quartet.

A colored waiter with a thin mustache and black shoes so
shiny they reflected light appeared and addressed Leo. 'Can I
help you?'

'Yes,' Leo said, and nodded at me.

'A martini please, no olive, and just a touch of vermouth,'
I said.

'Our house brand is Gordon's. Will that be acceptable?'

I was about to say yes, but Leo spoke up. 'Do you have
any Tanqueray?'

'We are fortunate to have several cases still, yes sir.'

'Then the lady will have that,' Leo said. 'I'll have a
manhattan with Glenlivet, please.'

'I'm sorry, sir, but we have no British whiskeys at all. Would
Jack Daniel's Black Label suffice?' I waited with baited breath
to hear if Frank Sinatra's favorite drink would meet Leo's high
standards.

'I suppose,' Leo answered.

Leo had demonstrated his sophistication and wealth to his
satisfaction, I hoped, because I had no patience with that sort
of thing. A real sophisticate wouldn't need to show off to a

waiter; he would be self-confident like Joe, who despite being poor knew more about music, art and books than Leo Maxwell ever would, even if he couldn't afford Jack Black.

At this point I was so curious as to why Leo Maxwell had invited me out I almost asked him outright.

Our drinks came, and when I sipped mine I understood why people were willing to pay for expensive liquor. My martini was wonderful. I wondered how much a pint of Tanqueray cost.

Leo leaned back in his chair, crossed his legs and sipped his manhattan.

'So,' he said, 'tell me, what kind of work do you do?'

'I'm a file clerk,' I said. 'I work for the government, just like everyone else in this town.'

'A file clerk,' he said. 'Just a file clerk, then. You seem . . . well, different from most government girls. More serious.'

I shrugged. 'I'm a thirty-year-old widow. Does that answer your question? You could have just asked me how old I am.'

He leaned toward me across the table. 'Louise,' he said, 'I can tell that I've started this evening off all wrong. I'm sorry. Can we begin again? I won't be pretentious, I promise.'

'I'm just wondering why I'm here, Leo. That's all.'

He sipped from his manhattan and reached across the table with his other hand, covering mine. 'Look,' he said, 'I get tired of talking about money and parties all the time. You're an attractive and interesting person. I don't meet girls like you very often.'

'Like what?' I pulled my hand gently out from under his.

'Who have jobs and are interested in something other than society.'

'What about Gloria? Where does she fit in?'

'Her marriage is unhappy and I need a wife with money of her own.'

'So it's a business arrangement.'

'I'm fond of her and she's fond of me. We'll do fine together. Let's stop talking about Gloria. Besides, you have a beau too, the man you were at the Baron Steuben with. Am I correct?'

'He is out of town on business. Indefinitely, I'm afraid.'

'Gloria will be in Chicago until after Christmas. Why should

you and I sit at home and sulk when we can go out and have
some fun?' He leaned toward me and lowered his voice.
'Besides, we were both in the Baron Steuben when a dead
man was found behind the bar. That sort of thing doesn't
happen very often.'

'No, it certainly doesn't.'

'You're a good friend of that policeman, aren't you?'

The interrogation had begun.

'Sergeant Harvey Royal is a personal friend, yes, but that
doesn't mean I know any more about the murder than you do.'

'Oh, please,' he said. 'Sure you do. I'm so curious about
it. I heard that Stinson was the custodian for the German
embassy. That's on my street, for heaven's sake!'

'He was, since the early thirties. I mean, he was an American,
not a German. The Swiss kept him on when the Germans left,
figuring he had experience with the building.'

Leo beckoned for the waiter. 'We'd like another drink and
to move to our dining table now,' he said.

The waiter nodded and pulled out my chair. We progressed
– that was the word that came to my mind – down three steps
into the dining area of the Pall Mall Room, where the waiter
seated us along the wall near one of the mirrored pillars. I
slipped into the banquette seat while Leo took the chair
opposite.

We sipped our second drinks while looking at the menu.

'Would you like me to order for you?' Leo asked. 'You
haven't been here before, have you?'

I prefer to choose my own dinner, but Leo had spoken with
no condescension in his voice and I did hope to get some
information out of him, so I decided to appear docile and
womanly. 'Yes, please,' I said.

While Leo ran his eyes down the menu I wondered if my
neighborhood liquor store stocked Tanqueray.

'Only one beef dish on the entire menu,' Leo said, glancing
up at me. 'I'll be glad when this war is over and a man can
get decent prime rib again. But the special is excellent, I've
had it before.'

A new waiter appeared to take our order.

'Malcolm,' Leo asked him, 'is the venison fresh?'

'Yes, sir,' he said. 'We received a box of fresh game packed in ice from New Hampshire this morning.'

'Then we'll have the venison ragout with currant jelly and chestnut purée. Are the oysters fresh also?'

'The chef selected them at the Central Market himself.'

'We'll have the oysters Bienville to start.'

'Yes, sir,' said the waiter with a slight nod, and glided away.

'Back to the murder, Louise. I understand Sergeant Royal considers us all to be suspects? Not just witnesses?'

I chose my words carefully. I didn't want to say anything that Sergeant Royal and Miss Osborne wouldn't want me to share.

'Yes, we are all suspects. There just weren't a lot of people out and about that night. Remember what the weather was like?'

'Cal must have seen the body when he opened the bar. Why didn't he call the police?'

'He was terrified. He wanted to wait until the bar closed.'

'But that scruffy bus driver just had to go looking for a bottle of whiskey.'

'Yeah, and you saw the rest of it.'

The waiter brought us our appetizer. I hated most seafood but I loved oysters. I'd rarely had them when I lived on the coast in North Carolina, and then they were fried. These were sort of puffy, obviously baked on the half-shell, seated in a bed of salt. I took a bite.

'Good, huh?' Leo said, noticing my expression. 'Never had them before?'

'No,' I said. 'They're delicious! What's in them?' While I waited for his answer I slid another hot, creamy oyster into my mouth.

'Let's see,' Leo said. 'The sauce is made of mushrooms, shallots, cream, butter, wine and breadcrumbs. Poured over the oysters, then browned. It's a New Orleans recipe, actually, from Antoine's. I watched our cook prepare it once.'

'They are wonderful.' I deeply mourned the last bite I took and watched the waiter take the plate away with sorrow. When Joe came back from wherever he was I'd fix them for him.

The waiter had left behind an inch-thick wine list. Leo went through it page by page, his brow furrowed to show his concentration. 'Any particular wine you'd like?'

'I don't know a thing about wine. And I'll only have a glass anyway. Otherwise I might fall asleep.'

Leo beckoned to a sommelier, who came over to the table to take his order. That had been a revelation to me, too, when I came to Washington, that when you went out to eat at a nice restaurant you often had more than one waiter. 'We'll have this Burgundy,' Leo said, pointing to the wine list. The sommelier nodded and took the wine list when he left the table. I still had some of my second martini left and sipped on it, thinking about those oysters. Leo sat quietly, twirling his empty highball glass around in his hand.

Our dinner came. I'd had venison before many times and it was often tough if not cooked properly. This had been marinated in red wine and garlic and grilled until just medium. It was tender and savory, not gamy at all.

I poked around the chestnut puree with my fork.

'Try it,' Leo said. 'You won't be sorry.'

I wasn't. It tasted sort of like roasted sweet potatoes and walnuts spiced with nutmeg and pureed with cream.

When I cleaned my plate I noticed with delight that the dishes were decorated with tobacco leaves and Sir Walter Raleigh's coat of arms.

Our waiter cleared our table and brought us coffee and the dessert menu. I remembered to reapply my lipstick, as Ada had advised me to do.

After browsing the menu for a few minutes Leo tossed it on the table. 'Awful choices,' he said. 'Pear crumble, tapioca pudding and apple and bread pudding. Do you mind if I smoke?'

'I don't smoke myself, but I don't mind if you do. And I don't want any dessert.'

'I'd think a girl from North Carolina would smoke. Don't you grow a lot of tobacco there?'

'Acres of it, but smoke makes my throat awfully sore.'

Leo lit a Marlboro with a match from the matchbook embossed with the words 'The Raleigh Hotel' left on the table in a crystal ashtray. When his eyes moved from the burning tip of his cigarette I saw the mask slip from his face just as if he'd pulled off a real mask. He wasn't any longer a genial dining companion but a spoiled playboy with a mean streak.

'You know,' he said, flicking cigarette ash into the ashtray, 'breaking and entering is a serious offense.'

'Pardon me?'

'You know what I'm talking about.'

'I don't, and I don't like your tone of voice, either.'

'I saw you come down the fire escape behind the German embassy. How did you get inside? What were you doing?'

I decided to turn the tables on him and see what happened.

'I had a very bad day and too much to drink at the Baron Steuben. No one was on guard at the embassy and I walked around outside and just for the hell of it tried the back door. It was unlocked and I went inside and wandered around. There were lots of huge empty rooms. I came to my senses and left. That's it.'

'I could turn you in and you'd go to jail,' he said.

I leaned across the table toward him, equally tense. 'I don't think so.'

'You don't?'

'I've already told Harvey Royal what I did, and he'll cover for me. He owes me a favor. Plus, you have no idea what government agency I work for. For all you know I could be J. Edgar Hoover's personal secretary. Leave me alone. I did nothing but wander around the inside of an abandoned house while under the influence. Why are you interested? That's what I want to know. Your father was practically a Nazi, wasn't he? Why didn't you call the police right away? Why didn't you tell me you'd seen me when I met you on the sidewalk? You must have a reason, and I bet it's not a good one.'

I saw him hesitate before telling me the truth. 'I wanted to know how you got inside because there's a lot of money hidden there.'

'That's just a rumor,' I said. 'But unless you want me to tell the police that you wanted to know how to get inside the German embassy so you could burglarize it you'd better keep your mouth shut about me.'

The waiter came to refill our coffee cups while we sized each other up.

'One more question,' he said once the man had moved away.

'You can ask whatever you want, but I might not answer you.'

'Why did you come down the fire escape when you went in the back door?'

I took a final swallow of coffee.

'When I decided to leave I found the back door locked. Scared me witless, not knowing who'd locked it. All the downstairs windows were nailed shut. I'd seen the fire escape from outside, so I crept upstairs, found the right room and clambered down it. After I got away and calmed down I figured that maybe the caretaker had checked the doors routinely, found one left open and locked it, and I just missed running into him.'

'Then you ran into me.'

'What luck.'

'Sarcasm isn't becoming in a woman. Especially one in your position.'

'I'd like to go home now. Dinner was delightful, the company less so.'

Leo didn't say a word, just stubbed out his cigarette and called for the chit.

In silence we claimed our coats at the cloakroom. Once outside Leo stopped the valet from going to pick up his car.

'I'll get it,' he said. 'Mrs Pearlie and I need the walk. It's in the usual lot?'

'Yes, sir,' the valet said, handing over the keys to Leo.

Leo took me firmly by the arm and led me down the street and then around the corner toward the back of the hotel. It occurred to me to run – I was sure I could outrun him – but I doubted he'd try anything, and I needed a ride home.

We turned into a parking lot. Under the shaded streetlights I spotted Leo's car. We both walked around to the passenger side. But instead of opening the door for me, Leo grasped me by my upper arms, hard, swung me around and shoved me up against the door.

I was livid. I hated to be bullied by anyone, especially a man as nasty as Leo Maxwell.

'Let go of me!' I said. 'Right now!'

'You tell me something first,' he said. 'Have you got the keys?'

'What keys?'

'The keys to the German embassy. I want them.'

'Are you crazy? Why would you think I'd have the keys! What a stupid idea.'

'Al killed Floyd Stinson for those keys. And then left town. I figure he gave them to you before he left, and you used them to get into the embassy and look for the money. But the caretaker got between you and the back door, so you had to go out the fire escape.'

'You fool,' I said, even though I'd once thought the same way. 'Al is dead. Someone found his body under the Taft Bridge yesterday. He'd been dead for two days, so he never got out of town. You're not the first one to think of Stinson's keys either, but Sergeant Royal told me the police found his keys in his room and returned them to the Swiss legation. Don't you even think of reporting me to anyone! How do I know you weren't the person in the embassy with me that night? Maybe you waited around for me after you locked the back door. Your family was close to the Germans for years; how hard would it be for you to have picked up a set of keys? Turn me loose, right now, or I'll mention my new theory to Sergeant Royal.'

Leo didn't release me. Instead he tightened his grip on my arms, really hurting me, and leaned into me until I felt his breath on my face. 'You modern girls are such bitches,' he said. 'Wait until the soldiers get back from the war. You'll all be back in the kitchen, where you belong. Men will be doing the men's work again.'

'What would you know about men's work?'

I didn't care that Leo clenched his teeth and hissed at me in anger but I did mind that his body moved closer to mine, and as his grip tightened even more my defense training kicked in. I couldn't use my hands but shifted to one side, threw all my weight behind the blade of my right foot and, sliding my foot down his shin as a guide, slammed my heel on to his foot. Leo howled with pain and released me, dropping to the ground and grasping his foot. If I'd done my job well he'd have at least one broken bone.

I kicked my shoes off, grabbed them up and ran as fast as I could back around the block to the front of the hotel. After a pause behind a bush to catch my breath and put my shoes back on, I walked sedately up to the front door. The valet looked at me in surprise.

'My date and I had an argument,' I said to him. 'Would you please call a taxi for me?'

ELEVEN

I leaned up against the door of my boarding house while I searched for my key to the front door. It was nearly midnight and I was bone-tired. My taxi had been held up by a messy accident on Pennsylvania Avenue that involved two cars and a truck full of vegetables coming into town from the country. After the taxi dropped me off I'd slipped on the icy sidewalk and landed on my hip. It hurt, and I'd have a huge bruise tomorrow.

My key wouldn't turn in the lock. It must be frozen. Jiggling didn't help. I thought about walking around the house to knock on Dellaphine's basement bedroom window. She or Madeleine could let me in the kitchen door, but I hated to wake them. I knelt on the frigid doorstep, put my mouth over the keyhole, inhaled deeply and blew my warm breath into it. When I tried the key again it engaged and I stepped into the house.

Rather than turn on a lamp I reached into my purse for my flashlight and followed the circle of light up the stairs. The heat had been turned down for the night so I didn't take my coat off. In my bedroom I quickly stripped and pulled on long underwear, flannel pajamas and two pairs of socks, stopping long enough only to hang up my dress. My stockings were ruined; I'd laddered them running shoeless back to the hotel after my altercation with Leo, so I pitched them into the trash can.

I went into the bathroom but didn't bother to brush my teeth or remove my make-up. I was too tired even for those simple tasks. But once in bed, under a mountain of blankets, I couldn't sleep. Everything that had happened to me since Joe and I had stopped in at the Baron Steuben for a drink last Saturday kept running through my head. Witnessing the discovery of Floyd Stinson's bloody corpse was just the beginning of a weeklong nightmare made worse when Joe left town and I didn't get to see him or talk to him beforehand.

I no longer remembered exactly what I had told Miss Osborne, what I had told Sergeant Royal (or rather not told him) or what I had told Mavis Forrester and Leo Maxwell about the case. Or when, for that matter. I'd lost track of my lies, although most of them were lies of omission rather than outright ones, but I was too tired and confused to care. On Monday, when I went in to work, I would give Miss Osborne a complete report. She would tell me what I was allowed to tell Sergeant Royal, and I would report to him. Then I intended to wash my hands of the entire affair. Al was dead. I was still not convinced he'd murdered Stinson, but it wasn't my job to clear his name, and there was nothing I could do for him that I hadn't done already.

'Don't look at me like that,' Ada said. 'I'm may not be much of a cook but I'm capable of removing a plate of fried Spam and waffles from the warming oven.'

The kitchen was the warmest room in the house, so Ada and I were enjoying a late morning cup of coffee at the kitchen table. Phoebe and Dellaphine were at the Western Market buying groceries for the week with our ration books and the morning newspaper sale ad. The men, Milt and Henry, were in the lounge listening to the news on the radio.

For once I had slept later than Ada. It was almost eleven o'clock in the morning when I made my way downstairs, the latest I had slept in years. Since Dellaphine didn't cook on Saturdays Phoebe had fixed breakfast and saved me a plate, bless her. In a most un-Ada-like rush of domesticity, Ada laid the table in front of me with napkin, knife and fork and brought me the plate of waffles and Spam. She even went into the pantry to get the maple syrup.

'You're being quite the housewife,' I said, as I took a bite of Spam. It was crunchy, just the way I liked it. 'What are you planning to do today?'

'Rehearse,' she said. 'It's too cold to go shopping.'

Ada was an accomplished musician. When she practiced I could hear her through the wall that separated our bedrooms. She played with the Willard Hotel house band, which was more than half female now. I wondered if she would be able to keep her job after the war when the men came home. She'd take a huge pay cut if she had to go back to teaching the clarinet instead of performing. She didn't seem to worry about her future after the war, though, not the way I did anyway.

'And what are you going to do?' Ada asked me. 'Read, as usual?'

'No, I'm going to the zoo.'

'You're joking. In this weather?'

'I need to clear my head. Besides, the new gorilla baby might be on display.'

'You're a queer girl, Louise.'

The zoo was almost deserted. It was strange to see it on a Saturday afternoon without throngs of people crowding the park and queuing at the various animal houses. I guessed it was just too cold and people were still worried about catching the flu. This was all right with me, I wanted to be alone anyway.

I'd bundled up in long underwear, corduroy trousers and a thick sweater under my coat. With my gloves and a scarf wrapped around my head I was comfortable, but the brisk walk from the bus stop to the ape house warmed me up even more. As I passed the seal and beaver ponds I saw the animals frolicking happily in frigid water. Or rather, the seals were frolicking and the beavers were working industriously on yet another dam. A couple with two children bundled up so that you could see only their eyes watched their antics.

In the ape house there were no other spectators but me. The animals were sensibly inside, in their viewing cages, avoiding the cold. The ape family seemed half asleep. Even Sultan was curled up in a straw nest, his eyes half open while one of his 'wives' groomed him. I was disappointed that the baby, Daudi, and his mother, Eshe, weren't on display yet with the rest of the gorillas.

'Do you believe in evolution?' a familiar voice asked me. I jumped, and turned with one hand over my heart.

'You startled me,' I said. 'I didn't hear you come in.'

Mavis Forrester stood behind me, enveloped in her mink coat with her hands deep in her pockets.

'Sorry,' she said, gazing at Sultan and his family. 'I was just thinking, I'm sure we're related to apes. Look at their eyes and their expressions. What do you think?'

'I don't really know. Every time I come here I think how like us the apes are. But I was raised to believe in Genesis word for word.'

'Adam and Eve and everything?'

'Yes. Weren't you?'

'I didn't go to church.'

'Oh.' I hadn't attended church since I'd been in Washington but I'd spent a lot of time as a child in church or at church. I'd read about the theory of evolution but hadn't given it much thought.

'I'd prefer a gorilla to lots of people I know, wouldn't you?' Mavis asked.

'Well, gosh, maybe,' I answered. I didn't know what to make of this odd conversation. 'Quite a coincidence to run into you here.'

'It's not a coincidence.' Mavis continued to stare at the gorillas while she talked with me. Her eyes seemed unfocused. Then she turned and stared directly at me, as if she was seeing me for the first time.

'I went to your house,' she said. 'I wanted to talk to you. Your landlady told me you were here.'

'How did you know where I lived?'

'I'm a librarian. I can find anyone's address.'

'Well, what is it you want to talk about? Do you want to go to the café and get a cup of coffee?'

'No, this is a good place.' Her eyes swept over the empty room. 'There's no one else here.'

'Tell me what this is all about, Mavis,' I said.

Mutely she pulled a hand out of one of her deep pockets and showed me the object in it. A tiny silver clown with an ivory face. The one I'd noticed missing from the cocktail table in the drawing room of the German embassy. She had been the intruder the night I wandered the embassy; she had stolen the clown and the cigarette lighter and she must have been the person who'd locked the back door, trapping me inside.

She must have had a key. How?

A key. For the first time I focused on an obvious fact, that there were bound to be many sets of keys to the embassy. How would the Swiss have known how many there were? They would have accepted whatever they were given by the Americans, who would have confiscated them from all the previous occupants of the embassy. But what about the Americans who worked there? Floyd Stinson, the custodian, would have kept his set, but he was still employed at the embassy.

Who else might have had a key – legitimately, that is? Other than the obvious people. Perhaps staff who didn't live there? Like Stinson. Or maybe a cleaning woman! The Germans wouldn't have brought a cleaning woman from Germany. They would have hired a local person to clean. Just as they hired Floyd Stinson as custodian. A cleaning woman might have a key to the back door, where the kitchen and service areas were located. And I remembered Sergeant Royal telling me that Mavis' mother was a cleaning woman, and how remarkable it was that Mavis had come so far up in the world.

Mavis held the clown up for me to see.

'It's so pretty, isn't it? I don't think I'll sell it yet; I don't need the money.' She gently pushed the clown back into her pocket.

'What else have you stolen?' I asked.

'Lots. Ever since the Germans left I've been going to the embassy. Mostly during bad weather, when the army guards huddle under the portico to smoke. You would be surprised what the Germans left behind.' She stretched out her hand to show me the diamond dinner ring on her right hand. 'In one of the bedrooms I found a little jewel case in a dresser drawer under a telephone book. The German woman who left it behind when our government evacuated the German embassy must have been distraught to forget it. I sold another ring and a couple of bracelets but kept this.' She turned her hand to admire the ring. 'I've found money and more jewelry, and items like the clown. That was my mistake, taking things in plain view. Floyd Stinson noticed. He figured out it was me. He knew my mother when she worked at the embassy. I used to come to the embassy sometimes with her. When he started to play chess with Al Becker at the Baron Steuben he recognized me.'

'So that was the mansion you talked about? Where you had to sit still all day and read?'

'That was it.'

'And your mother had a key to the back door. I'm surprised the Germans gave her one.'

'The butler gave it to her. He didn't like being awakened as early as she arrived. She had to get most of her work done before the Germans woke up and came downstairs because they didn't like to see the help. She died of pneumonia in 1939 and I found the key in the pocket of one of her uniforms when I was cleaning out her closet.'

I found myself gripping the guardrail hard with both hands, as if I couldn't trust myself to stay standing. Why had Mavis followed me here? Why had she confessed all this to me? What did she plan to do? She clearly had a mental disease.

'What do you want from me?' I asked.

'I went out to eat last night with friends, at the Bistro Français. The maître d' told me you were asking questions about me. Where I was on Tuesday. As if I needed an alibi. I can't have that, Louise. I must stop you. You do understand, don't you?'

My gut knew I was in danger before I did, seizing up into a painful, hard knot. Mavis was threatening me. But before I tried to escape her I wanted to know the truth about what she'd done.

'Mavis, did you kill Stinson?'

'I had to. He was going to turn me in to the police. I talked him into meeting me at the bar before he did. I hinted that I was going to give him my key and some of the stolen stuff I still had to return to the embassy.'

'You knew the key to the back door of the Baron Steuben was outside above the door.'

'Sure. Everyone regular knew it. We saw that moron Cal reach for it often enough.'

'I don't understand why you hid the body behind the bar.'

'I thought the bar would be closed because of the weather.

Instead that damn kid came in to open up. You should have seen him. He was so frightened he blubbered. I promised him that I'd give him three hundred dollars if he helped me hide the body until I could get rid of it. He'd already turned on the lights and the neon sign so we didn't have time to get it away.'

'The two of you dragged Stinson's corpse behind the bar where no one could see it but the barkeep. You ditched the knife and the bloody coat and tablecloth, then came back into the bar to keep an eye on Cal.'

'It was a good plan. Should have worked. Would have except for Walt.'

'You know that Al Becker was suspected of Stinson's murder and that he killed himself because of it, don't you? You're responsible for the death of two people!'

'He didn't kill himself. I killed him. I ran into him on the Taft Bridge after I had dinner last Tuesday night with friends. He challenged me. Apparently Floyd had told him he was suspicious of me, asked him if he remembered my mother and me. So I had to kill him too. I just tipped him over the rail and threw his suitcase over after him. I'm very strong, you know. I swim at the Y almost every day after work.' She was stronger than Cal, that's for sure, strong enough to stab Floyd Stinson with the knife she found in the storage room.

Mavis wouldn't have confessed Al's murder to me unless she planned to kill me too.

I glanced back at the door to the ape house. No one appeared. Mavis and I were still alone.

'Look,' I said to her. 'The best thing for you to do is surrender yourself. Sergeant Royal will figure out it was you eventually.'

'I don't see why,' she said. 'He's sure Al killed Floyd. And Floyd is dead and can't correct him. He thinks Al committed suicide. If you're not around to tell him about me, how will he know?'

Mavis pulled a Luger out of another pocket. It was a 'Black Widow', so called because of its black pistol grip. She pointed it directly at me. 'I'm sorry,' she said, 'but I'm going to have to kill you too. Then I'll be safe.'

I had to use all my strength to keep from trembling and present a calm front.

'Mavis, you'll be caught. Someone will have seen you. Sergeant Royal is a very good detective. Three murders, you'll hang!'

'I don't see why. The zoo is deserted. I haven't seen a single guard. They're all somewhere warm drinking coffee. The keepers won't appear until it's time to feed the animals. I came in through the eastern gate and I'll leave the same way. No one was on duty there.'

I licked my dry lips. 'Someone will hear the shot.'

'From inside a concrete building? I doubt it. Besides, I'll be long gone. When the doctors at your autopsy dig the bullet out of your body they'll see it came from a Luger. I stole it out of a desk drawer in the office at the embassy. That'll confuse them good. On my way out of the zoo I'll toss the gun in the creek. I won't steal anything from the embassy for a while. I've got lots of money stashed away. Then when I go back I'll stay away from anything in plain sight. That was my mistake. I should have stuck to drawers and cabinets.'

Just then Sultan stretched and let out what could only be called a bellow, startling us both. He lumbered over to the bars of his cage to check us out. Mavis was distracted long enough for me to grab at the gun. I tried to wrench it from her hand, but she was very strong and I couldn't get it away from her. With every ounce of strength I could summon I pulled her close to me and kneed her in the stomach. She cried out and doubled over long enough for me to turn around and break for the door. I'd worn saddle shoes today, thank God. A shot exploded and ricocheted off the floor at my feet, so close I could feel bits of the cement floor spraying my ankles. Another shot drove me away from the exit and toward the door to the back room where Eshe and Daudi were housed.

The shots drove Sultan wild. He screamed, beat his chest and threw himself at the bars of his cage while his family cowered in a corner. Climbing up the bars with all four limbs he clung there and howled again, rattling the bars so hard the entire cage wall shook. I found the door to the room where Eshe and Daudi had been isolated and tried to wrench it open, but the lock was jammed. Like Al had when we visited earlier,

I jiggled the doorknob roughly. But while I worked at it I kept my eyes on Sultan, who was still enraged. The entire wall of bars shuddered as he threw himself against it.

Mavis had picked herself up off the floor and, still clutching her gut with one hand, apparently terrified that Sultan might break out of his cage, aimed the Luger at the enraged gorilla.

'Don't!' I screamed. 'Don't shoot him! He can't hurt you! He can't get out!'

Mavis heard me and swung the gun toward me. The door gave way under my hand and swung open. I rushed into the room, turned and slammed the door shut. Lungs burning, I leaned against the door to pull myself together. I heard a guttural snort and turned to see Eshe staring at me from behind the bars of her cage. Daudi clung to her back.

'Hi, there,' I said, struggling to keep my voice from wavering. 'Don't be afraid. Remember I was here before with your friend Al? I'm not going to hurt you or your baby.'

Eshe didn't believe me. She looked quite nervous and pulled her baby son even closer to her.

I heard footsteps outside the door and quickly grabbed a chair to jam under the doorknob. The doorknob began to turn as Mavis tried to get at me. I'd trapped myself here in this tiny room and didn't see any way to get out, except to keep Mavis on the other side of the door. I didn't think I could do that for long.

I cast about the room for a weapon and saw a thick rod balanced on top of a pile of feedbags. Picking it up, I noticed the brass battery case and two metal prongs sticking out of one end. It was a cattle prod, used to keep Eshe back when she was being fed, I supposed. I grabbed it up. I doubted it would be much use against a Luger but it was better than nothing. Where the hell were the zoo guards? Even in freezing weather they should be checking on the animal houses.

Eshe moved to one side of her cage and I noticed a door behind her, a low door with just a knob to open it. The door that led to the outside enclosure. It was secured to a wall hook to keep Eshe from opening it while Daudi was small, but just with a bit of rope. On the other side of the door I heard Mavis fling her weight at it. The chair I'd propped up against the doorknob scraped across the floor. I didn't doubt that, unless by some miracle a guard appeared, Mavis would break through and shoot me.

'It's OK, girl,' I said to Eshe, as I moved toward her cage. 'I'm not going to hurt you.' Eshe didn't take her eyes off me, her arms wrapped around Daudi, who watched me curiously.

It took just a second for me to unlatch the cage door. I pointed the prod at Eshe and she shot to the corner of her cage and cowered, with her body between her baby and me. I hoped I wouldn't have to use the prod against her.

'I don't want to hurt you. Stay back,' I said to her, feeling foolish about reassuring her as if she was a person.

I dug my knife out of my pocketbook and cut through the rope, pushing the outside door open. I was in the outdoor cage in no time. But I wasn't alone. Sultan was outside too.

The silverback was still furious. Jumping and bellowing, he glared at me. I guessed he'd come outside into the cold to get away from the gunshot only to find himself face to face with another unpredictable human. I held the cattle prod close to my side, thinking that if he saw it in my hand it might enrage him further. It would me. I'd seen farmers use electric prods on cattle and hogs before and it was obvious they were painful.

From the other side of Eshe's cage door I heard her chatter and Mavis' voice. I couldn't understand what Mavis said but she must be inside the holding room with Eshe and Daudi. All she had to do was crawl through Eshe's cage and through the door to the enclosure and I – and Sultan – would be trapped here with her. I didn't see how I could escape. Of course there was an exterior door on the outside cage for the keepers to use, but I could see from where I stood it was fastened with a lock so huge it looked medieval.

Then there was the door from the outside cage to the big viewing cage inside the ape house, where the rest of Sultan's family remained. It wasn't a door, actually, just a heavy plastic flap, and if I used it I'd find myself penned in with three gorillas instead of one.

Sultan had stopped howling, his head cocked toward the door to Eshe's cage, listening to her whimpers. He dropped to his knuckles and edged forward. Since I was standing right next to the door I moved too, working my away along the cage wall away from the door and Sultan. The volume of Eshe's chattering increased and now I could hear Daudi whimpering. Mavis must be in their cage with them. I backed further away from the door and raised the cattle prod. Sultan saw it and paused, baring his huge teeth at me.

Mavis opened the door and crawled out into the cage, mink, Luger and all. For a second the absurdity of my predicament overcame me and I almost laughed out loud. I was trapped in a gorilla cage with an angry silverback gorilla and a woman wearing a mink coat who wanted to kill me. The three of us created quite a tableau. Mavis standing by one door brandishing a Luger, Sultan on guard in front of the entrance to the room where his family was and I, armed with a cattle prod, slinking along a wall to get away from both of them. The going wasn't easy. The enclosure was crowded with rocks, branches, a climbing structure and a small rubber pond built to provide some sort of distraction for the gorillas, but about as far from resembling their African home as I could imagine. There were some human toys scattered about too, a couple of balls and, of all things, a baby carriage. On the far side of the cage was the feeding area and the heavy door to the outside.

Mavis had the gun trained on me, but kept an eye on Sultan. The gorilla crouched, watching us both. The muscles of his huge body rippled, as though he was ready to pounce but couldn't decide which one of us to tear apart first. I thought of screaming, but I knew that then Mavis would shoot me – and maybe Sultan too, if he attacked her.

'If you use that gun now people will come running,' I said. 'Just give up, please. Give me the gun. We can get inside, away from Sultan, and call the police.'

Mavis just laughed at me. A loud, ringing laugh that started Sultan prancing.

'Don't be silly,' she said. 'I'm a rich woman. I have no intention of losing anything that I have, not one thing, do you understand me? I'm going to kill you and escape. When I shoot you all I have to do is get out through the mother gorilla's door into the ape house. From there I'll be out of the park before the first police car turns into the front gate. It'll be fun watching your dimwit friend Sergeant Royal try to figure out why you were shot with a Luger in a gorilla cage.'

The three of us stood there like gunfighters daring each other to draw first. Which was fine with me. The longer Mavis hesitated the more likely it was that someone, anyone, would come along, see us and sound an alarm. But she was a smart woman, and she knew she needed to act quickly.

I saw the resolution cross Mavis' face just in time to fling myself to the ground, banging my head hard against the iron bars of the gorilla cage as I fell. I heard the bullet whiz by me overhead as I hit the concrete floor. The next one would get me for sure.

As I lay on the cold concrete, dizzy from the knock on my head, I heard Sultan roar. Then another gunshot, and Sultan bellowed in pain. But he wasn't down, he kept roaring, and then I heard Mavis scream in terror. Before I blacked out entirely I heard a police whistle sound and the pounding of feet running from all directions.

'Is she alive?'

'Yes. I think she just bumped her head. She's not bleeding anywhere and her pulse is OK.'

I heard Mavis sobbing a distance away. I struggled and failed to open my eyes.

'The other woman?'

'Sultan about ripped her arm off, but we've got a tourniquet on her. The ambulance is on the way.'

'Sultan?'

'Bleeding from his shoulder, but inside raising Cain. The vet's coming with a tranquilizer gun.' I was glad to know Sultan was alive; I could care less about Mavis. I struggled to sit up and speak.

'Ma'am, you need to lie still.'

'Has someone called the police?' I asked.

My eyelids felt like they were weighted down with anvils, but I forced them open. A zoo guard and a civilian, I supposed a visitor to the zoo, were bent over me.

'You want Sergeant Harvey Royal,' I said. 'It's his case.'

* * *

The other customers in the zoo café studiously avoided staring at me. I didn't blame them. It wasn't every day that two women and a gorilla mixed it up the way Sultan, Mavis and I had.

Sergeant Dickenson had gotten me away from the gorilla cage before the press and photographers arrived, saving me from exposure on the front page of tomorrow's newspapers. He'd wrapped a blanket around me and brought me to the zoo restaurant where a doctor who'd been touring the zoo examined me and said that, except for a goose egg over one ear, I was uninjured. My head hurt and if I moved it I saw stars, but the cup of hot chocolate warmed my hands and tasted wonderful. Dickenson had gotten me a piece of pie too, but I hadn't eaten any yet.

Harvey came in the entrance and limped over to our table, sitting down next to me.

'Would you bring the car around, please?' he asked Dickenson, who nodded and left.

'You need to eat some of that pie,' Royal said to me. 'You look very pale. Have you had lunch?'

'No,' I said, 'no I haven't. But I'm not hungry.'

Royal picked up a fork and cut off a piece of pie and held it up to my lips.

'Eat,' he said, 'or I'll take you to the hospital. You're probably in shock and you need sugar.'

I took the bite of pie he offered me. 'You can't take me to the hospital,' I said. 'You know I work for a government agency. I need to stay out of this.'

'Then you'd better eat something.'

'At least give me the fork so I can feed myself.'

He was right. After I'd polished off the pie I did feel better.

'Is Mavis going to live?' I asked.

'Not in the long run,' he said. 'She'll hang. But she was still breathing when they put her in the ambulance.'

'Sultan?' I asked.

Royal raised an eyebrow. 'You mean the gorilla? I think he'll be OK. I heard one of the zookeepers say the vet dug a bullet out of his shoulder. That's one big damn animal. I saw the size of his teeth when he was lying there on the concrete.'

'You should see him when he's angry.'

In the car on the way home I found myself growing sleepy. Dickenson was driving; Royal was in the back seat trying to keep me awake so he could pump me for information.

'Look, I'll come by tomorrow when you're feeling better and take a statement,' Royal said. 'But please, just give me the high points.'

'OK,' I said. 'Mavis Forrester's mother was a cleaning lady at the German embassy in the thirties. She had a key to the back door. After she died, Mavis found it when she was cleaning out her things. She used it to steal from the embassy after the German legation left.'

'That took nerve.'

I shrugged. 'She knew her way around. She was careful, and the Swiss believed the place to be secure. The residents had been evacuated so quickly that they left plenty behind. I mean, the Swiss were supposed to protect the building and its contents for the duration of the war. She stole jewelry, money, even the Luger. She sold most of what she stole.'

'That's how she could afford her own apartment.'

'And a mink and an expensive social life. Anyway, she got overconfident and started stealing valuable objects that were in plain view. Stinson noticed they were missing and concluded someone was getting into the embassy, and it had to be someone with a key.'

'Why didn't he notify the Swiss?' Royal asked.

'I don't know,' I said. Another lie. Stinson was working for OSS and didn't want to attract attention to the embassy. 'Anyway, he ran into Al Becker at the Baron Steuben Inn one night. They remembered each other from when Al worked at the embassy too. Then I suppose one of them, or both, recognized Mavis. She had often accompanied her mother to work.

'So Stinson contacted Mavis and told her of his suspicions. I don't know what his plan was, maybe he was just going to ask her to stop burglarizing the place and give him her key. Anyway, she agreed to meet him at the Baron Steuben, hoping to come to some agreement with him. A key to the back door was hidden on the ledge above the door – all the regulars knew it. Mavis killed Floyd.'

'She's one strong woman.'

'And has no conscience at all. She's got ice water running in her veins. She didn't hesitate to drive that knife right into Stinson. Cal almost ruined the setup. He came in to open the bar. But you know Cal: he was terrified. She offered him money to hide the corpse behind the bar until closing time, when she could dispose of it. She left through the back door and got rid of the knife and bloody clothes. Then she returned to the bar and ordered coffee with a shot of brandy. And was cool as a cucumber when Walt found the body. She killed Al when she found him skipping town, tossed him over the railing of the Taft Bridge and threw his suitcase after him. In broad daylight. Just because he might know Stinson suspected her of breaking into the embassy.'

'Why did she come after you?'

'I ran into her at the Baron Steuben Wednesday night. It had been a rough day and I had a couple of drinks. I guess she didn't like the questions I asked her. Or me checking on her alibi for the night Al was murdered.'

We pulled up to the door of 'Two Trees', but Royal took a firm grip on my arm, preventing me from climbing out of the car.

'You're lying to me,' he said. 'There's more to all this, I know there is. And you will tell me.'

We held a staring contest that ended in a draw. He continued to keep me from getting out of the car.

'Talk,' he said. 'Louise, our friendship won't survive this, and I'll find out the truth anyway.'

I couldn't tell him. I couldn't tell him Stinson worked for OSS, searching the old embassy for intelligence. If I did he'd have to tell the Swiss and that would be the end of that. The repercussions would be ugly.

'I haven't lied to you,' I said. 'Have I told you everything? No. I can't. But I can tell you that you've got the right killer. And if you put any more of the story together I will verify what I can. That's all I can do.'

Royal released me. I didn't like the look in his eyes at all. The man was angry. And sad, too. The lame, tired old cop had trusted me. I suppressed an urge to take his hand and fought back tears.

'I'm sorry,' I said to him. 'I had no choice. There's a war on.' I stepped out of the car on my own and walked as confidently as I could down the sidewalk to 'Two Trees'.

AUTHOR'S NOTE

After Germany's surrender in 1945, the US State Department seized the German embassy. When it was searched officials found three million American dollars in cash. The building remained vacant until it was demolished on November 24, 1959.